My E...
Story...

BECCI MURRAY

ISBN: 978-1-913944-08-7
Published by Llama House Children's Books

☠ THE PIRATES OF ☠
MONKEY ISLAND

A STORYQUEST BOOK BY
BECCI MURRAY

For Harriet Jeffery,
a StoryQuest Superstar

CHOOSE THE PAGE - UNLOCK THE ADVENTURE

ISBN: 978-1-913944-06-3
Published by Llama House Children's Books

Welcome to your StoryQuest challenge, the book where YOU are in charge of what happens and YOU are the star of the adventure.

Start your quest on the first page, where your challenge will be explained. At the end of each chapter you'll find two options – choose a page to decide what you want to do next.

As a bonus feature, every StoryQuest book has a SPECIAL CHARACTER hidden amongst the pages. Find the character, and they'll give you a STORYQUEST STAR. This will help you unlock the ultimate ending to your adventure.

There are SO many different paths and SO many different endings – some are good, some are bad, some are happy, some are sad. Which will you choose? Will you complete the challenge? And where will your story end?

Good luck, intrepid StoryQuester, and happy reading!

The seaside is lovely at this time of year. You've built a sand-castle, you've eaten an ice-cream the size of your head and you're just taking a quick paddle when two people in a rowing-boat appear on the distant horizon.

"Avast ye!" the man calls out. "Oi'm Jimmy Smallhands and this be me trusty crewmate, One-Eyed Brenda. Be careful in these 'ere waters, matey, for there be *pirates* about."

"Yargh!" cries the enormous woman.

There's a rat on her shoulder. It waves a tiny cutlass and accidentally slices off half of her moustache.

"Erm, okay," you reply. "But I think *you're* the pirates, aren't you?"

Jimmy Smallhands nods.

"Aye, matey, that we are. But we be *good* pirates, see? We be the kind of pirates what feeds yer bones to the fishes then takes our grannies out fer a nice pot o' tea and a slice o' cake."

"Pieces of cake! Pieces of cake!" squawks the rat.

"But if you're pirates," you say, "where's your

ship?"

"Alas, matey, the Martha Rose were stolen by a fearsome band of scurvy villains called...*the Pirates of Monkey Island!*"

He shudders when he utters their name, as if someone covered the words in slime and dropped them down the back of his shirt.

You scratch your head with confusion.

"So, what you're saying is...*pirates* stole your pirate ship?"

"Aye, but not just any pirates. *Monkey*-pirates! They pilfered our ship then they thieved our treasure chest too." Jimmy Smallhands sighs heavily. "We were really lookin' forward to eatin' those chocolate coins, weren't we, Brenda?"

"Yargh!"

"You had a treasure chest with *chocolate* coins in it?" you gasp.

"Aye, matey," replies the man, "us pirates can't go a single day without eatin' chocolate, or else we gets the rumbly tummies and that ain't nice fer no-one."

One-Eyed Brenda's stomach grumbles like custard sliding down a plughole. He's right – that wasn't nice for anyone.

"Oh, dear," you reply. "What are you going to do

about it?"

"What're we gunna do?" repeats Jimmy Smallhands. "We're gunna row to Monkey Island and steal it back again, that's what we're gunna do. Trouble is, those scurvy monkey-pirates made the rest of our crew walk the plank and the two of us ain't got no chance of findin' them coins on our own, so..." One-Eyed Brenda picks you up by the arm and plonks you down in the boat. "Welcome aboard, matey!"

"What?!" you cry. "But I can't join your pirate crew!"

"Oi don't see why not," shrugs Jimmy Smallhands.

"Because I'm on holiday," you say. "Because I'm meant to be playing crazy-golf after lunch. Because *I'm not a pirate!*"

"No need to worry about that," smiles the man. "Me and Brenda wouldn't take ye to Monkey Island without the proper piratey equipment. We've got three items to 'elp with yer quest."

"What, like a cannon and a cutlass, or something?"

Jimmy's smile flickers.

"Well, no, but we do 'ave this fine pair of oars. And One-Eyed Brenda's got a telescopic eyeball she can take in and out, so we got that too, ain't we, Brenda?"

"Yargh!"

"But best of all, we got *this*." Jimmy picks up the rat and drops it onto your lap. It smells of wee. "I mean, it ain't no parrot, but it might just come in useful fer somethin'. So, matey, what do ye say? Will ye come with us to Monkey Island and 'elp steal back our chocolate coins?"

Brenda's eyeball spins full circle then fixes on you like an all-seeing pickled onion.

"Well, all right," you say. "But only if Brenda stops looking at me."

"Swashbucklin'!" cheers Jimmy Smallhands. "And remember, we must find the coins without bein' captured by the monkey-pirates or we'll all be walkin' the plank before sunfall," and with a pull of the oars, you row out across the rolling ocean on a quest to find the stolen treasure.

Your StoryQuest has begun. Turn to page 24 to start your adventure.

"Quick, Brenda," you say, "show Big Baboon Bob your telescopic eyeball!"

The woman skids to a halt. She spins around to face the monkey-pirate, takes hold of her eyeball and pops the thing out of its socket.

PWUCK!

The pupil zooms in and out like a tiny telescope.

WHIR! WHIR! WHIR! WHIR!

Big Baboon Bob stares for a moment in horror, then he squawks like a parrot and runs in the opposite direction.

Swashbucklin'!

"Wow, Brenda, that was great!" you say, as your crewmate shoves her eyeball back into her face. "Let's get to the shipwreck before he comes back."

On the eastern shore of the island, the land is rocky and steep. The huge wreckage of the old vessel looms on the coastline like the washed-up carcass of an ancient sea-monster. Two pieces of its great mast have snapped off and landed in an X shape on what's left of the decking. You'll need to take a closer look if you want to search for the treasure.

There are two ways to get up to the deck: you could climb the fallen rigging on the outside of the boat, or go in through a hole in the starboard side.

How will you get up to the mast?

To climb the rigging on the outside of the shipwreck, turn to page 33.

To go in through the hole, turn to page 44.

You decide to use one of the oars to slice through the net, so you take out the item and hack at the rope as if cutting it with a saw.

Hm, that doesn't seem to have worked, so you use the oar like a hammer and whack the rope as if nailing it into a wall. Nope, that hasn't worked either.

Slowly, you raise the oar over your shoulder and strike the net in a karate chop motion.

"Hi-ya!"

But your aim is a little off. The fat end of the wooden paddle slices through the wrong rope and the three of you plummet towards the ground like mammoth acorns, where you land in a prickly hawthorn bush.

A spine gets stuck in One-Eyed Brenda's bottom. You help her limp back to the boat where you carefully remove the thorn, after which you head back to the mainland to recover from the ordeal of seeing Brenda's backside.

Go back to the start of the book to try again, or turn to page 62 to make a different choice.

"Yes, please, I'd love to stay for a snack," you reply, and Robinson Cuckoo passes you half of Mr Coconut's head.

"You always did like chicken chow-mein, didn't you, Marjorie?" says the man. You watch in horror as he bites a chunk from the coconut shell and crunches it up like a boiled sweet. "Just wait 'til you see what's for pudding."

The hairy man goes to a small chest in the corner of the room. He opens the lid and an army of crabs crawls out.

He places one of the critters onto the table. You notice a star in one of its claws. There's a picture of your crewmates on one side and the number 16 on the other.

"A StoryQuest Star!" you cheer. "Wow, thank you, Robinson Cuckoo!"

The man wrinkles his nose.

"It's not a star, Marjorie. It's lemon meringue pie." It's not. It's *definitely* a StoryQuest star. "Just memorise the number then hand it over to your crewmates when you've finished your quest to unlock the ultimate end to your story."

"Awesome," you say. "Shall I put it in my pocket for safe-keeping?"

"If you want," shrugs Robinson Cuckoo, "but if I were you, I'd shove it down my trousers like any other sane person. Now, if you'll excuse me, Marjorie, I have a crème brûlée to attend to. Good seeing you again," and the woolly man goes back to his barrel and pulls down the lid.

Congratulations – you've found the StoryQuest Star!
Turn to page 64 to go up to the fallen mast of the shipwreck.

You launch the rat across the jungle. Captain Fluffy-Beard catches it mid-flight and looks curiously down at its whiskery face.

"Shiver me timbers," he gasps, "you're the scariest-lookin' monkey oi ever did see."

"He's not a monkey," you explain, "he's a—"

"Oi knows a monkey when oi sees one," snaps the captain, "and oi'm recruitin' this little lad as the newest member of me monkey-pirate crew. His piratey name shall be Whiskery Pete and if you three bald monkeys don't join too, I shall feed Whiskery Pete to the sharks. Whadda ye say to *that*, me hearties?"

As the person who just threw the rat, you feel responsible for the mess he's in, so you agree to join Captain Fluffy-Beard's crew and are known forever more as Baldy Lobster-Legs of Monkey Island.

Rude.

Go back to the start of the book to try again, or turn to page 40 to make a different choice.

10

You march bravely onto the plank as if walking along a diving board at your local swimming pool and jump elegantly into the cool…

SPLODGE!

Oh, dear.

The tide is out at this time of day, so instead of landing in water, you've splatted into the muddy sand of the eastern coast. It takes five hours to dig yourself free, by which time the Howler Twins have captured your crewmates and eaten all of the chocolate coins for themselves.

Go back to the start of the book to try again, or turn to page 83 to make a different choice.

One-Eyed Brenda walks bravely towards the plank.

"Time to swim with the fishes, ye scabby codfish!" cries the first Howler Twin.

"Yer a cabby codfish!" laughs the other. "Yo, ho, ho, ho, hooo!"

Brenda's eyeball zooms in on a tiny crack in the ship's deck.

WHIR! WHIR! WHIR! WHIR!

The huge woman places her feet on the crack, and jumps.

SMASH!

The ship is so rotten that the floor gives way and the whole group of you tumble down through the wreckage as the old vessel splits in two.

Five pairs of feet hammer into the muddy sand beneath the boat like darts in a corkboard.

SPLODGE!

SPLODGE!

SPLODGE!

SPLODGE!

SPLODGE!

It's a bit of a result for One-Eyed Brenda – she doesn't have to walk the plank after all. But it also means you'll be stuck here until the tide comes in and washes you out of the sand, by which time the other monkey-pirates will have realised you're here and scoffed the chocolate coins for themselves.

Go back to the start of the book to try again, or turn to page 64 to make a different choice.

You climb down from the wreckage and onto the shore.

"Brenda," you say, "as there aren't any coins on the shipwreck, would you mind using your telescopic eyeball to search for another X?"

"Yargh!" replies One-Eyed Brenda.

A gentle whirring sound comes from inside the woman's head, as her eyeball spins in its socket.

WHIR! WHIR! WHIR! WHIR!

The pupil pops out like a tiny ice-cream cone.

POP!

And zooms in on the other side of the island with a rusty, *CREEEEEEEEAK!* It's the most disgusting thing you've ever seen or heard in your life, but it's also pretty awesome.

The woman points to the south of the island.

"Brenda says there be another X on top o' Big Face Rock," explains Jimmy Smallhands. "But Big Face Rock is difficult to climb and dangerous too."

Brenda points to the west of the island.

"She says there also be an X in the window of an ancient ruin," says Jimmy, "but an evil spirit guards the buildin' and chases away anyone who goes near it. I gotta tell ye, matey, I don't much fancy visitin' *either* place, but oi'll leave the choice up to ye."

Which X would you like to look at next?

An evil spirit? No, thanks! I'll go to Big Face Rock.
Turn to page 31.
An evil spirit? Cool! I'll go to the ancient ruin. Turn to page 78.

"Shiver me timbers!" cries Jimmy Smallhands. "Ye found the StoryQuest Star! Time fer a treat, matey."

With a small wink, he hurls the star into the ocean. It hits a wave and the sea turns to gold, as an enormous ship *made of chocolate* rises up from the blue.

"That's the tastiest ship I've ever seen!" you gasp.

"And it be *your* ship," smiles Jimmy. "Ye can sail the seven seas in this beauty. Ain't that right, Brenda?"

The woman's eyeball zooms in on the humungous lump of floating chocolate.

"Y…y…y…" she stammers. But the word doesn't want to come out. "Y…y…y…*you should just eat it!*"

One-Eyed Brenda's cheeks turn pink.

"I think that's a brilliant idea, Brenda," you laugh. "But that's a lot of chocolate for one person. Does anyone want to help me finish it off?"

And Brenda replies, "Yargh!"

Congratulations, you've finished your quest and found the ultimate end to your adventure. You're a StoryQuest legend, matey. Swashbucklin'!

Untying the knots is almost impossible. Captain Fluffy-Beard has pulled them so tight with his tiny hands, you can't get a grip on the string.

"This be a job fer someone with bloomin' small fingers," smiles Jimmy Smallhands, and in a blur of tattoos, he unravels the string until a big hole appears in the net. Swashbucklin'!

One by one, you crawl through the hole and sit on the nearest branch. Captain Fluffy-Beard said the chocolate treasure isn't buried in the jungle, so you scan the area for other places to search.

To the north of the island, there's a small lagoon with a large X hovering over the pool. Or there's a battered shipwreck to the east, with a broken mast that has fallen in the shape of an X.

Where would you like to go next, me hearty?

Let's visit the shipwreck. Turn to page 82.
Let's go to the lagoon. Turn to page 53.

You leave the shark-infested waters and head towards the shipwreck on the eastern coast of the island, where the land is rocky and steep. The huge wreckage of the old vessel looms on the coastline like the washed-up carcass of an ancient sea-monster.

Two pieces of its great mast have snapped off and landed in an X shape on what's left of the decking. You'll need to take a closer look if you want to search for the treasure.

There are two ways to get up to the deck: you could climb the fallen rigging on the outside of the boat, or go in through a hole in the starboard side.

How will you get up to the mast?

To climb the rigging on the outside of the shipwreck, turn to page 33.
To go in through the hole, turn to page 44.

18

You lie on your stomach and reach out to One-Eyed Brenda with the oar. She grabs hold and clutches it tightly, as you pull her out of the sand.

"Think yer clever, do ye?" growls Stinky Silverback Shelly. "We'll soon see about that. 'Ave a whiff of these bad-boys, me hearties."

The gorilla raises her arms and a terrible pong wafts over the beach. It hits your face like a wave, stinging your eyes and clouding your brain, until your eyes roll back in your head and you pass-out on the sand.

Crumbs! You've been thwarted by the smell of Stinky Silverback Shelly's armpits and your quest has come to a rather stinky end. But you rescued your crewmate and for that you are a truly magnificent human.

Swashbucklin'!

Go back to the start of the book to try again, or turn to page 35 to make a different choice.

19

You climb up to the crow's nest for a better look at the island. The view from here is fantastic. You can literally see right across to the other side of the—

SNAP!

Uh oh. The pole holding the crow's nest must have been damaged when the ship crashed and the extra weight has snapped it in two. You plummet towards the deck like a falling anchor, crash through the rotten wood and drop into the ship's galley.

You land next to a very hairy man.

He's carving a face into a coconut.

"How good of you to drop in on us," he says. "Oh dear, you seem to have hurt yourself. Have a drink out of Mr Coconut's head. It'll make you feel much better."

But drinking out of Mr Coconut's head doesn't make you feel better, so your crewmates wrap you up in bandages like an Egyptian mummy and send you back to the mainland to recover.

Go back to the start of the book to try again, or turn to page 47 to make a different choice.

You start the long climb to the top of Big Face Rock, pulling yourself onto the chin, over the bottom lip and up towards the biggest nose you've ever seen in your life.

The tip of the nose is round and smooth. It's going to be tricky to hold on if you try to climb over it, but there's a dim light shining out through the rock's left nostril. It could be a secret tunnel leading up to the peak.

Will you climb over the nose to reach the summit, or do you want to crawl up the nostril?

I want to crawl up the nostril, please. Turn to page 74.
No-one *wants* to crawl up a nostril. I'll climb over the nose please. Turn to page 51.

Making a shark costume is easy. You take some palm tree leaves and sew them together with long lengths of grass, then you whittle a set of teeth from a coconut and – *hey presto!* – you have yourself a cunning disguise.

As you enter the lagoon, the shark's head rises up out of the water.

"Why, hello," grins the giant fish. "Welcome to the Monkey Island lagoon. We don't get many giant slugs around here."

"I'm not a slug," you reply. "I'm a shark like you. See? I've got the teeth and everything."

"My dear," says the shark, "ten out of ten for effort, but you most definitely do *not* have the teeth."

She flashes you her razor-sharp set of gnashers. She's right. Your teeth are rubbish compared to hers.

"Okay, so, I'm not a shark," you say, your voice trembling. "But I made this costume because I want to search the lagoon. You see, I'm on a quest to find some missing chocolate coins and I think they might be under this X."

"There's no chocolate in here," says the shark. "If

there was chocolate in my lagoon, I'd be eating it right now, because I'm absolutely *starving*."

The shark moves towards you and her jaws open, but a big hook drops suddenly into the water. It catches hold of your palm-leaf fin and lifts you out of the pool.

As the shark sinks miserably into the shadowy water, you look up to see a hideous monkey face staring down at you. Crikey, it's Big Baboon Bob! He's one of Captain Fluffy-Beard's crew!

How are you going to escape?

I'll keep pretending I'm a shark and scare him away.
Turn to page 46.

I'll bite through the fishing-line with my coconut teeth and scarper. Turn to page 81.

You row out across the shimmering ocean until a small island appears on the distant horizon.

"That be Monkey Island," says Jimmy Smallhands, as your rowing-boat enters a crescent-shaped cove. "If we wants to find the missin' coins, we'll 'ave to look fer where X marks the spot."

You hide the boat in a patch of long grass and scan the white beach. Someone has made a big X out of seaweed on the sand.

But beyond the cove, a palm tree jungle looms in the distance like an angry storm cloud. Two of the trunks are taller than the others and they've crossed over to form an enormous X in the sky.

Where would you like to look first, StoryQuester?

I'll check out the X on the beach please. Turn to page 35.

I'd like to go to the palm tree jungle. Turn to page 42.

Leading your crew to safety, you push past the monkey-pirates and run out of the ancient ruin. Captain Fluffy-Beard chortles as he runs upstairs and holds up a chest full of chocolate coins to the X-shaped window.

"Is *this* what ye were lookin' for?" grins the captain. He unwraps one of the delicious coins and shoves it into his pretty little face. "Well, we're gunna eat the whole bloomin' lot and you'll all have rumbly tummies fer the rest of yer lives," and his motley crew laugh hysterically.

You look sadly down at your feet as the sun lowers in the evening sky. It casts an orange glow over the island, silhouetting the ancient ruins against the reddening horizon. Sunlight pours through the upstairs window of the roof-less building. It casts the shadow of an X onto the ground in front of you.

Your heart races.

"X marks the spot," you gasp, hardly able to believe your eyes. "Quick, Jimmy Smallhands, pass me one of those oars."

Hurriedly, you dig down into the soft ground until

25

the tip of the oar hits the lid of a wooden chest and with trembling hands you open it. A hundred or more golden chocolate bars are glistening in the fading sunlight. Crikey! This treasure must have been buried here by another pirate crew!

One of the Howler Twins appears in the doorway of the ruin.

"Captain!" he yells. "They be findin' buried chocolate bars, Captain, and they're much bigger than our coins! Come quick, come quick!"

Okay, StoryQuester, this could be your final choice – will you take your loot and run away from the monkey-pirate crew, or will you tell those nasty bullies exactly what you think of them?

I'll tell the nasty bullies exactly what I think of them.
Turn to page 66.
Let's grab the treasure chest and leg it! Turn to page 37.

You gulp down the water and put the shell back on the table. At once, a grubby-looking man with torn clothes and more hair than a yak bursts out of an old barrel.

"Marjorie!" he warbles, as if all his Christmases have just come at once. "I've poured that water every day for fifty years, Marjorie, in the hope you'll pop over for dinner." He pulls a silver tray from behind his back. It has a live sea-snail on it. "Amuse-bouche?"

You eye the snail and the snail eyes you.

"Erm, no, thank you," you reply. "Sorry, but...do I know you?"

"Oh, Marjorie, you're such a card. It's me! Robinson Cuckoo! I've waited half a century for you to arrive, Marjorie, with no-one to talk to except Mr Coconut over there. It's a wonder I haven't completely lost my marbles." He pulls a jelly-fish out of his trousers. "Strawberry trifle?"

Robinson Cuckoo washed up on Monkey Island when his ship crashed into the rocks. You'd feel mean telling him you're not Marjorie, so instead you play along and apologise for your late arrival.

"Sorry to keep your waiting, Robinson," you say, "but I'm afraid I can't stay for dinner right now. You see, I'm on a quest to find some missing coins."

The man looks sadly over at the empty dinner table. He puts the jellyfish on his head and sighs.

"I understand, Marjorie," he says, miserably. "But can't you stay for just one little snack? I really have been ever so lonely."

He rips the coconut man's head off his driftwood shoulders, smashes it open on the table and offers you the biggest half. Do you want to share Mr Coconut's head with Robinson Cuckoo, or will you make an excuse and go up to the deck?

This guy's a nutjob. I'll make an excuse and go up to the deck. Turn to page 64.

I'd love to eat Mr Coconut's head! Turn to page 8.

You find a strand of seaweed from the shoreline and throw one end of it to Brenda. The woman grabs hold. She clings on tightly as you and Jimmy pull with all of your might, and—

SNAP!

The seaweed breaks.

Brenda sinks further into the ground and with a muffled, "Yargh!" she completely disappears.

"Har, har, har!" laughs Stinky Silverback Shelly. "That were more fun than firin' cannonballs at dolphins."

You hear footsteps coming from underneath the quicksand. It sounds like One-Eyed Brenda has landed in some kind of secret chamber. Will you try to find her or head towards the palm tree jungle to continue your quest?

Leave my crewmate behind? No way! Let's try to find her. Turn to page 88.

I'll go to the palm tree jungle and continue my quest. Turn to page 40.

"Quick, run for the stairs!" you call out to your crew, and you dash up the dusty old steps.

Below the X of the broken window frame, there's a treasure chest. Brenda's stomach gurgles at the sight of it.

"There be our chocolate coins!" cries Jimmy. "There be our scrummy treasure!"

Captain Fluffy-Beard and his crew appear at the top of the stairs.

"Think yer real smart, don't ye?" he snarls. "But tell me, ye scurvy scoundrels, how do ye plan to get past *us* with your loot?"

The monkey-pirates have you cornered. They tie you up and chomp down every last one of the coins, then they send you back to the mainland with nothing more than a chest full of wrappers.

That's a rum deal when you're so close to finishing your quest. Make another choice to complete your challenge.

Go back to the start of the book to try again, or turn to page 85 to make a different choice.

Big Face Rock is a big rock that looks like a face and it was named by someone with no imagination.

Two enormous boulders stare down over a craggy nose as you gaze up at the X on the very top of the rock's head. Someone will have to go up there to look for the chocolate coins.

"Brenda," you say, "would you mind climbing to the summit of Big Face Rock to look for the treasure?"

One-Eyed Brenda curls up in a ball on the ground and quivers with fear. You take that as a, no. It looks like either you or Jimmy Smallhands will have to make the treacherous climb instead.

Yes, please, I'd love to climb Big Face Rock. Turn to page 21.
No, thanks, I'll let Jimmy climb it. Turn to page 49.

"Jump for the creeper!" you call out to your crewmates.

The other end of the plant is attached to a wooden beam on the ceiling and the old roof creaks as the three of you shimmy up to the rafters.

"You're going to break that," says the little monkey ghost, matter-of-factly. "If you break that ceiling, I'll be really cross with you."

A huge crack snakes across the beam. It won't hold you up for much longer. You'll have to lighten the load so the roof doesn't collapse, but how?

I'll let go of the creeper to lighten the load and face the little monkey ghost myself. That sounds like the brave thing to do. Turn to page 72.

Let's drop the rat. Turn to page 85.

The rigging looks fairy sturdy, so Jimmy and Brenda keep look-out from the shore as you haul yourself up to the deck.

The old wreckage is creaky and damp, its sails are tattered and torn, the crow's nest has actual crows in it and the cannons are covered in barnacles.

You walk towards the broken mast to investigate the X. There's an old rum barrel directly below the cross, but you search inside it to find nothing more than seasnails and crabs. There's not a single chocolate coin to be seen on the whole ship.

Turning to leave, you see two identical monkey-pirates standing behind you. It's the Howler Twins, Captain Fluffy-Beard's first and second mates.

"What're ye doin' on our shipwreck, ye mangy varmint?" snarls the first twin.

"Yer a mangy varmint!" laughs the second. "Yo, ho, ho, ho, hooo!"

You try to think of a convincing answer to the monkey-pirate's question. But you can't think of one, so instead you reply, "I'm delivering pizzas."

You're not sure why you said that.

"You can't deliver pizzas 'ere," says the first Howler Twin. "It's only monkey-pirates what are allowed on Monkey Island, ye hornswaggling barrel-bellied blighter."

"Yer a hornswaggling barrel-bellied blighter!" laughs the second. "Yo, ho, ho, ho, hooo!"

"And if ye ain't a monkey-pirate, you'll 'ave to walk the plank, ye filthy parrot-faced rapscallion."

"Yer a filthy parrot-faced rapscallion! Yo, ho, ho, ho, hooo!" The second twin lowers his furry eyebrows. "What's a pizza?"

How are you going to escape from the Howler Twins?

To tell them you're a monkey-pirate, turn to page 47.

To walk the plank then swim back to shore, turn to page 87.

The closer you get to the seaweed X, the deeper your feet sink into the ground. You stop to investigate the muddy sand.

"I don't be likin' the look of this," says Jimmy Smallhands. "I reckons that X be a trick. I reckons we be headin' for quicksand."

The two of you hurry to the side of the beach, but One-Eyed Brenda has already gone on ahead. She sinks into the sand like a stone through jelly, until only the top half of her body is sticking up out of the ground.

Suddenly, from the other side of the X, a gorilla appears. She's wearing a red bandana and beating her chest like a drum.

It's Stinky Silverback Shelly, one of the monkey-pirate crew!

"Captain Fluffy-Beard said you'd come lookin' fer those chocolate coins we pilfered," snarls the gorilla. "That's why oi made that seaweed X on the beach, to trick ye onto the quicksand. You'll never find where we've *really* hidden the treasure, ye motley scallywags."

Oh, no! One-Eyed Brenda has fallen for Stinky

35

Silverback Shelly's trick and she's sinking fast. You can't walk on the quicksand to pull her out, so you'll have to use an item to reach her.

You could try using one of the oars, or grab a string of seaweed from the shoreline. Which item do you think will work best?

Let's use one of the oars. Turn to page 19.

I'll try using a strand of seaweed. Turn to page 29.

The three of you take hold of the chest full of chocolate bars. Wowsers, it's really heavy! Jimmy Smallhands clutches his back and drops his side of the box.

"Me back! Me back!" he cries, holding your arm to keep himself upright. "I've only gone and put me back out!"

The treasure chest lands on One-Eyed Brenda's foot.

"YAAAAAARGH!"

With your crewmates injured, you lift the chest on your own. But it's too heavy for you to run with and the monkey-pirates are soon snatching it out of your hands.

You were so close to completing your challenge, matey, but it looks like you'll have to stand up to those mean monkeys if you want to finish your quest.

Go back to the start of the book to try again, or turn to page 25 to make a different choice.

You launch the rat across the jungle. Captain Fluffy-Beard catches it mid-flight and looks curiously down at its whiskery face.

"Shiver me timbers," he gasps, "you're the scariest-lookin' monkey oi ever did see."

"He's not a monkey," you explain, "he's a —"

"Oi knows a monkey when oi sees one," snaps the captain, "and oi'm recruitin' this little lad as the newest member of me monkey-pirate crew. His piratey name shall be Whiskery Pete and if you three bald monkeys don't join too, I shall feed Whiskery Pete to the sharks. Whadda ye say to *that*, me hearties?"

As the person who just threw the rat, you feel responsible for the mess he's in, so you join Captain Fluffy-Beard's crew and are known forever more as Baldy Lobster-Legs of Monkey Island.

Rude.

Go back to the start of the book to try again, or turn to page 42 to make a different choice.

"I'd love to do some yoga with you," you say to the golden eagle.

After trying out a few poses, you sit next to the great bird and meditate as the sun melts into the distant horizon.

"Relaxing, isn't it?" he says.

"It really is," you reply. "In fact, I feel as if I could almost...fall...ZZZZZZZZ!"

Oh, dear. You've fallen asleep on the summit of Big Face Rock and you don't wake up until the monkey-pirates have stuffed every last one of the chocolate coins into their furry little mouths.

Go back to the start of the book to try again, or turn to page 51 to make a different choice.

The palm tree jungle is alive with the sound of tropical birds and animals. As you pick your way through the undergrowth, a little face pops out from the foliage. It's *so* fluffy and cute! Its cheeks are like two tiny pom-poms, its nose is no bigger than a button and its sparkling blue eyes are glistening like the ocean itself.

"Hello, there, little guy," you say to the adorable creature. "Aren't you a sweet little—"

The face leaps out of the bush, grabs hold of you by the collar and pins you to the ground.

"Scurvy parrot-faced rapscallion!" snarls the creature. The animal's delicate eyelashes flutter like two butterflies. "What're ye doin' on my island, ye mangy son of a sea-dog?"

Jimmy Smallhands starts quivering like a jellyfish.

"It's Captain Fluffy-Beard," he stammers. "He's the leader of the monkey-pirates and the cutest villain to ever 'ave lived."

Captain Fluffy-Beard wants to know what you're doing on his island. You can't tell him you're here to steal back the treasure or he'll pummel you with his

40

sweet little fists.

What are you going to say?

I'll say we're on a banana hunt. Turn to page 69.

I'm saying nothing. Let's set the rat on him! Turn to page 10.

The palm tree jungle is alive with the sound of tropical birds and animals. As you pick your way through the undergrowth, a little face pops out from the foliage. It's *so* fluffy and cute! Its cheeks are like two tiny pom-poms, its nose is no bigger than a button and its sparkling blue eyes are glistening like the ocean itself.

"Hello, there, little guy," you say to the adorable creature. "Aren't you a sweet little—"

The face leaps out of the bush, grabs hold of you by the collar and pins you to the ground.

"Scurvy parrot-faced rapscallion!" snarls the creature. The animal's delicate eyelashes flutter like two butterflies. "What're ye doin' on my island, ye mangy son of a sea-dog?"

Jimmy Smallhands starts quivering like a jellyfish.

"It's Captain Fluffy-Beard," he stammers. "He's the leader of the monkey-pirates and the cutest villain who ever lived."

Captain Fluffy-Beard wants to know what you're doing on his island. You can't tell him you're here to steal back the treasure or he'll pummel you with his sweet little fists.

What are you going to say?

I'll say we're on a banana hunt. Turn to page 62.

I'm saying nothing. Let's set the rat on him! Turn to page 38.

The hole in the starboard side of the shipwreck is big enough for *you* but much too small for One-Eyed Brenda's bottom. Watching her try to squeeze through it is like watching someone trying to push a bouncy-castle through a drainpipe.

"Oi reckons me and Brenda should stay out 'ere on the shore," says Jimmy Smallhands. "We can keep a look-out and if we sees any monkey-pirates, we'll make a noise like a dolphin to let ye know. Ain't that right, Brenda?"

"Yargh!"

Thanking your crewmates, you climb through the hole. The inside of the wreckage smells damp and rotten. Sea crustaceans cling to the walls, crabs scuttle in and out of the woodwork, and the floor is slick with a carpet of green algae.

At the centre of the room, you see a table. Six plates have been laid out in front of the chairs and the silver cutlery has been polished until you can see your reflection in it. That's strange. Why are the knives and forks so shiny? And why do you feel like you're being watched?

You turn suddenly to see a man with a coconut head, driftwood arms and a body made out of stuffed palm-tree leaves at the far end of the table. He's been carefully tied together with plaited grass and a creepy smile has been carved into his face. Perhaps the monkey-pirates made him to scare you away from the treasure.

The fake man has a shell of fresh water on the table in front him. Searching for treasure is thirsty work and you'd like to take a sip, but you really should be getting on with your quest. Will you drink the water, or go upstairs to investigate the X?

I'll take a drink of water please. Turn to page 27.
I'll leave the water where it is and go up to the deck.
Turn to page 83.

"Rargh!" you say, showing the monkey-pirate your fine set of coconut teeth. "I'm a shark! Rargh, rargh!"

"Bloomin' barnacles!" cries Big Baboon Bob. "Oi've only gone and caught meself a tasty snack. Captain Fluffy-Beard loves a shark-meat sandwich. Just ye wait 'til he sees what oi got fer our supper."

You try to tell Big Baboon Bob you're not really a shark, but he's not listening – he's too busy putting you on the menu for tonight's monkey-pirate feast and covering you with garlic.

I guess your shark impression was just too bloomin' good. Rargh!

Go back to the start of the book to try again, or turn to page 22 to make a different choice.

"Ahoy, thar, me hearties!" you cry, in your best piratey voice. The Howler Twins look at each other with confusion. "Ye can't be makin' me walk the plank, for I be a monkey-pirate too, see? Splice the mainbrace! Man overboard! Shiver me timbers! Pieces of eight! Heave ho and walk the plank! Yo, ho, ho, ho, hooo!"

As monkey-pirate impressions go, it's not bad.

"Oh," says the first twin, scratching his furry head. "Why didn't ye say so? Oi suppose if ye be a monkey-pirate too, we'd better be lettin' ye go or Captain Fluffy-Beard will be terribly cross."

"Thanks very much," you reply. "I mean…too right, ye hornbucklin' swoggly-doggly sea-cucumbers!" and with a shrug of their shoulders, the Howler Twins leave the shipwreck.

Swashbucklin'!

You didn't find any treasure on the wreckage, so you'll need to search somewhere else for the coins. But there are no more Xs in sight. You could climb up to the crow's nest for a better view of the island, or leave the shipwreck and ask Brenda to use her telescopic eyeball for a good look around.

Which will it be, matey?

I'd like to climb up to the crow's nest. Turn to page 20.

I'll leave the shipwreck and ask Brenda to use her telescopic eyeball. Turn to page 89.

Jimmy Smallhands starts the long and dangerous climb to the top of Big Face Rock. He pulls himself over the chin, onto the bottom lip and finally climbs up to the stony moustache for a quick rest below the enormous nostrils.

"Is everything all right, Jimmy?" you call out.

"There ain't no way to get around the nose!" he replies. "Oi'm gunna 'ave to climb over it!"

"You can do it, Jimmy!" you shout. "We believe in you! Just go for it!"

"Yargh!" adds One-Eyed Brenda.

The rock's nose looks like a humungous turnip. Jimmy reaches for the end of it, but his hands are too small to hold on. His foot slips and he bounces down the side of Big Face Rock like a rubber ball, twisting his ankle and grazing his knee.

You and Brenda feel guilty for having encouraged your crewmate, so you take him back to the mainland for a doctor to bandage his leg. The treasure will have to wait for another day, but you're an awesome friend and that's much more important than any amount of chocolate.

49

Swashbucklin'!

Go back to the start of the book to try again, or turn to page 31 to make a different choice.

Your hands are just big enough to take hold of the huge nose and heave yourself onto the bridge. But the rock here is slippery and smooth. Your feet slide over the surface like ice – you're going nowhere fast.

Suddenly, the rocks starts to twitch. You're tickling it with your feet and the itching is too much to bear.

Big Face Rock wrinkles its nose as it tries to hold on to a sneeze. The creases make a ladder rising up to the peak. You place a foot into the bottommost wrinkle and scramble up to the summit.

There's the X! It's big, it's X-shaped and…it has *feathers*, for some reason.

"Namaste," says the feathery shape.

You frown. It isn't an X at all. It's a golden eagle, standing perfectly still with its legs apart and its wings held up in the air.

"Hello," you say. "I thought you were an X. I don't mean to be rude, but what are you doing?"

"Yoga," replies the eagle. "This, my friend, is what we yogis call a warrior pose. You should try it. It's very calming."

Would you like to do some yoga with the golden eagle, or get on with your quest?

I love yoga – let's do it! Turn to page 39.

This is a StoryQuest not a yoga retreat. I'd like to get on with my quest. Turn to page 58.

The lagoon is a small circle of still water with a faint smell of eggs. The X you saw is made out of two wooden bridges that cross over at the centre of the pool.

"If the chocolate coins be hidden 'ere," says Jimmy Smallhands, "they must be down there in the water."

"Yargh!" agrees One-Eyed Brenda.

A dark shape catches your eye from below the surface and a triangular fin slices through the murky water. It cuts across the pool like a knife as the head of a shark rises up from the pool.

Eek! These are *shark-infested* waters! And if the treasure's hidden beneath the bridges, you'll have to jump in.

Do you have a cunning plan to fool the sharks, or would you like to change your mind and investigate the shipwreck instead?

I have a cunning plan – I'll make myself a shark costume before I jump in. Turn to page 22.

That's not a cunning plan. I'll go to the shipwreck instead. Turn to page 18.

"I'd like Jimmy Smallhands to go first," you tell the Howler Twins, "because he looks like he'll float better than One-Eyed Brenda. No offence, Brenda."

"Yargh," shrugs the woman.

"Oi will be honoured to face the plank first, matey," replies Jimmy with a wink, and the monkey-pirates march him across the deck with his hands tied firmly behind his back.

You're surprised at how keen Jimmy Smallhands is to meet his watery fate. But then you notice his fingers are wriggling around and before you know what's happening his tiny hands slip free of the rope. He grabs the two terrible monkey-pirates by the tails and they yelp as he slings the pair of them over the side of the shipwreck and into the muddy sand below.

SPLODGE!

Swashbucklin'!

"I do be reckonin' that were your fault, ye mangy barnacle-brain," says the first twin to his brother.

"Oi'm a mangy barnacle-brain!" laughs the second. "Yo, ho— Hey, who are ye callin' a barnacle-brain, ye bloomin' tentacle-head?"

You untie One-Eyed Brenda and gather your crew near the X.

"I've looked all over this ship for the chocolate coins," you tell them, "but there's nothing here. We'd better find another X to investigate and fast, before the Howler Twins escape from that mud and cause any more trouble."

How would you like to search the island for more Xs?

I'll climb up to the crow's nest for a better view of the island. Turn to page 80.

I'll leave the shipwreck and ask Brenda to use her telescopic eyeball to search the island. Turn to page 14.

"Not to worry, matey," says Jimmy Smallhands. "You've finished yer quest and that's all that matters. And as a thank you fer all yer hard work, me and Brenda 'ave got a little surprise fer ye."

One-Eyed Brenda takes a mountain of gold chocolate bars out of the treasure chest and places them into your arms.

"Wow!" you gasp. "Is this all for *me?*"

"Aye," replies Jimmy, "it be your share of the treasure and oi reckons you've earned it. That there is a lot o' chocolate though, so make sure ye don't eat it before supper or it'll spoil yer appetite. Ain't that right, Brenda?"

The woman's eyeball zooms in on the heap of chocolate. Her mouth starts to water.

"Y…y…y…" she stammers. But the word doesn't want to come out. "Y…y…y…*you should eat it right now!*"

One-Eyed Brenda slams a hand over her own mouth and her cheeks turn pink.

"Thanks, Brenda," you laugh. "Do you really think that's a good idea though?"

And Brenda replies, "Yargh!"

Congratulations! You've completed your quest and
you're a pirating StoryQuest hero. Swashbucklin'!

If you'd like to read more StoryQuest adventures, take
a look in the back of this book.

"Thanks for the invite," you say to the golden eagle, "but I don't have time for yoga. You see, I'm on a quest to find some missing chocolate coins. I don't suppose you've seen any lying around up here?"

"I'm afraid not," says the bird. "But I was performing a downward dog this morning when I noticed a group of monkeys going into the ancient ruin with an old treasure chest. You might want to try there."

Thanking the eagle, you climb down to your crewmates and before long the three of you are standing in front of the ancient ruin. Above the doorway, there's a rotten window-frame. It forms a perfect X at the top of the building, so you step inside and head for a dusty staircase in the back wall.

One-Eyed Brenda stops in her tracks. She points a trembling finger over your shoulder and you turn to see a pale figure floating behind you.

Blimey, it's the evil spirit!

Except, it's not evil at all. It's a little monkey ghost with a cross look on her face.

"What're you doing in my ruin?" demands the

58

ghost. "Get out before I scare you away with my ghostly woo-ing."

GULP.

You'd really like to leave now, but you'd also like to search upstairs for the treasure. What are you going to do?

There's a creeper hanging down from the ceiling. Let's jump for it and climb away from the little monkey ghost. Turn to page 32.
I did enough climbing on Big Face Rock. Let's throw the rat at her. Turn to page 76.

You stop running and turn suddenly.

"Oh look, there's a bear!" you shout, pointing over Big Baboon Bob's shoulder.

Your acting skills are magnificent and the monkey-pirate panics. He spins full circle, waving his arms as if being chased by a wasp, before running away with his tail between his legs.

Swashbucklin'!

But suddenly you realise Jimmy Smallhands and One-Eyed Brenda are also vanishing into the distance. You forgot to explain your plan to them and you're such a talented actor they believed what you said about the bear, so they're running away as fast as their legs will carry them.

By the time you catch up with them, Big Baboon Bob has convinced the other monkey-pirates to set sail for a safer island and they've taken the chocolate coins with them. Drat that imaginary bear!

Go back to the start of the book to try again, or turn to page 81 to make a different choice.

"Quickly, run for the stairs!" you call out to your crew, and you dash up the dusty old steps.

Below the X of the broken window frame, there's a treasure chest. Brenda's stomach gurgles at the sight of it.

"There be our chocolate coins!" cries Jimmy. "There be our scrummy treasure!"

Captain Fluffy-Beard and his crew appear at the top of the stairs.

"Think yer real smart, don't ye?" he snarls. "But tell me, ye scurvy scoundrels, how do ye plan to get past *us* with your loot?"

The monkey-pirates have you cornered. They tie you up and chomp down every last one of the coins, then they send you back to the mainland with nothing more than a chest full of wrappers.

That's a rum deal when you're so close to finishing your quest. Make another choice to complete your challenge.

Go back to the start of the book to try again, or turn to page 76 to make a different choice.

"We're on a banana hunt," you tell Captain Fluffy-Beard. "Yep, we're just three banana-hunters and a rat out looking for some tasty yellow snacks. There are loads of them at the top of these two crossed-over trees, so if you don't mind, we'll just climb up and take a look."

The monkey-pirate narrows his eyes.

"Not so fast, landlubber," he says. "Oi'm a *monkey.* Don't you reckon oi'd know if there were bananas on this island?" He has a point. "And if you ain't 'ere for the fruit, I reckons you've come to steal me treasure."

Captain Fluffy-Beard wraps his tail around a small branch and pulls. The leaves on the ground shoot into the air as a big net scoops you up. It lifts you to the top of the tree, where you dangle helplessly with your crew like a rather strange-looking coconut.

The monkey-pirate captain howls with laughter.

"The chocolate coins ain't hidden in the jungle," he hoots, "and yer'll never find the right X by *hangin' around* in a tree all day. Oi'll let ye down in a week or two though…if you're lucky," and he scampers away through the trees with his little tail floating behind him like a pretty feather.

Oo, you'd like to boot that sweet little ball of fluffiness to the other side of the island. But first things first – how are you going to free your crew from this net?

I'll use an oar to slice through the string. Turn to page 7.

Let's untie the knots to open it up. Turn to page 17.

Leaving the galley, you climb up the small wooden staircase and step out onto the ship's deck. The sails are tattered and torn, the crow's nest has actual crows in it and the cannons are covered in barnacles. There's an old rum barrel directly below the X of the broken mast, but you search inside to find nothing more than seasnails and crabs.

There's not a single chocolate coin to be found on this whole bloomin' ship!

"Welcome aboard, ye scurvy stowaway," snarls a voice from behind you.

"Yer a scurvy stowaway! Yo, ho, ho, ho, hooo!" laughs another.

You turn to see two identical monkey-pirates standing behind you. Jimmy Smallhands and One-Eyed Brenda are with them and their hands have been tied up with rope.

Cripes! It's the Howler Twins – Captain Fluffy-Beard's first and second mates!

"We've captured yer crew and taken 'em hostage, the mangy sea-dogs," says the first monkey.

"They be mangy sea-dogs!" laughs the second

64

twin. "Yo, ho, ho, ho, hooo!"

"We're gunna make 'em walk the plank," says the first, pointing to a wooden board nailed to the side of the wreckage, "and *you're* gunna choose which one of 'em goes first, ye fish-faced hornswaggler."

"Yer a fish-faced hornswaggler! Yo, ho, ho, ho, hooo!"

Well, this is terrible. Not only do you have to decide which crew member will walk the plank first, but that monkey-pirate's laugh is *really annoying*.

Who will you choose to take the plunge first, matey?

I'll choose Jimmy Smallhands. Turn to page 54.

I'll choose One-Eyed Brenda. Turn to page 12.

You place both hands on your hips and peer down at the tiny monkey-pirate captain. He reminds you of a teddy-bear you used to have.

"Stop being so *mean!*" you tell him. The captain looks a bit confused. No-one has ever stood-up to him before. "*We* found this treasure, not *you*. What would your mothers say if they found out how horrible you are to your fellow pirates?"

Big Baboon Bob looks sheepishly down at his feet.

"She'd send me to bed with a good tellin'-off," he replies, "and she'd stop me pocket money for a month."

The Howler Twins chew at their bottom lips and their cheeks glow redder than Big Baboon Bob's bottom.

"Our mammy would say we've been very naughty monkeys," says the first twin, "because we ain't supposed to eat chocolate before supper."

"And we ain't allowed to cross the ocean on our own yet neither," adds the second.

You turn to Captain Fluffy-Beard and look him square in the eye.

"And what about you, Captain? What would *your* mother say if she knew about all the terrible things you've been up to?"

The captain folds his tiny arms and pouts.

"She'd say if oi steals any more chocolate, she'll send me parrot back to the pet-shop and lock me cannonballs in a cupboard." He stares glumly at your golden chocolate bars and sighs. "I suppose ye can keep yer treasure, and you'd better 'ave these too." Captain Fluffy-Beard tosses a bunch of keys to Jimmy Smallhands. "I didn't really make the rest of yer crew walk the plank," he admits. "I locked 'em up in me ship's dungeon. Well, in *your* ship's dungeon."

Swashbucklin'!

You hoist the treasure chest onto your shoulder and Brenda helps you carry it back to the ship, where Jimmy Smallhands releases the rest of your crew from their cells.

"None of us will 'ave a rumbly tummy with so much chocolate to eat," smiles Jimmy, "and it's all thanks to you. Ye be the best crewmate we ever did 'ave."

"Yargh!" agrees One-Eyed Brenda.

"You've finished yer quest and you've taught them monkey-pirates a lesson they'll never forget. I don't reckon they'll be pilferin' our treasure again any time soon. Tell me, matey, did ye find the StoryQuest Star fer us too?"

If you were given a StoryQuest Star by Robinson Cuckoo, turn to the page number you saw glittering on it when he handed the item over.

If you don't have a StoryQuest Star, you've still finished your quest and you're still awesome! Turn to page 56.

"We're on a banana hunt," you tell Captain Fluffy-Beard. "Yep, we're just three banana-hunters and a rat out looking for some tasty yellow snacks. There are loads of them at the top of these two crossed-over trees, so if you don't mind, we'll just climb up and take a look."

The monkey-pirate captain narrows his eyes.

"Not so fast, landlubber," he says. "Oi'm a *monkey.* Don't ye reckon oi'd know if there were bananas on this island?" He has a point. "And if ye ain't 'ere for the fruit, oi reckons you've come to steal me chocolate coins. Well, the joke's on you, matey, because the treasure ain't hidden in this jungle, so you're lookin' in the wrong—"

Suddenly, a trapdoor is flung open under Captain Fluffy-Beard's feet. The tiny monkey shoots into the air like very small, very furry rocket and lands in a thorn-bush with his tail up over his head.

One-Eyed Brenda climbs out of the hole where the captain once stood.

"Brenda!" cries Jimmy Smallhands. "You're alive! Are ye all right, me hearty?"

Brenda points to the hole in the ground.

Jimmy gasps.

"Brenda says she's found a secret underground tunnel," explains the man. "She says she landed in it when the quicksand swallowed 'er up. She says she don't reckon the monkey-pirates know about it. She says it goes right across to the other side of the island."

Crikey, that One-Eyed Brenda is a real talker.

Captain Fluffy-Beard squirms inside the thorn-bush. He's so angry about having been fired across the jungle that his fur is standing on end. He looks like someone just took him out of the tumble-drier.

"We should scarper before Captain Fluffy-Beard gets outta that bush," says Jimmy Smallhands. "But these monkey-pirates be quick on their feet, matey. Oi'm worried he might catch up with us."

One-Eyed Brenda has an idea. She climbs back through the trapdoor and beckons you into the underground tunnel.

"Great idea, Brenda," you say. "Let's get out of here," and the three of you climb inside.

When the trapdoor closes, the passage is thrown into darkness. Brenda's eyeball lights up like a torch. It illuminates the tunnel and you follow the path all the way to the other side of the island, where you climb out through a second trapdoor.

There's an X on either side of you. One lies over the top of a small lagoon and the other has been formed by the broken mast of an ancient shipwreck. Which X would you like to investigate first, StoryQuester?

I'd like to go to the shipwreck please. Turn to page 82.
I'd rather go to the lagoon. Turn to page 53.

You jump down from the creeper and land in front of the little monkey ghost.

"I told you to get out of my ruin," snaps the ghost. "Right, that's it, prepare yourself for a woo-ing. *WOOO-OOOO-OOOO—*"

"Stop that right now!" you say, sternly. "It's really mean to frighten people. This ruin doesn't belong to you and if I want to search it, *I will.*"

The monkey ghost's chin starts to wobble, she sniffs loudly and then a fountain of big, fat tears bursts out of her eyes.

"*WAAAAAAAH!*"

"Oh, no, please don't cry," you say, quickly. "I didn't mean to upset you."

"I thought frightening people was what ghosts are supposed to do," splutters the ghost. "What else can I do in this miserable old ruin?"

"Ye could play hide-and-seek," suggests Jimmy Smallhands, from up on the creeper.

The little monkey ghost's face lights up.

"I *love* hide-and-seek!" she smiles. "I'll count to twenty and you hide. Ready? Steady? Go! One, two, three, four…" and that's how you got stuck in an ancient ruin for a week playing hide-and-seek with a monkey ghost.

Go back to the start of the book to try again, or turn to page 32 to make a different choice.

The walls of the giant nostril are lined with moss. You take hold of the soft plant, pull yourself into the nose and climb until the glimmer of light turns into a gaping hole.

You can see the X on the top of Big Face Rock and…are those *feathers?*

Suddenly, the walls of the nostril start to tremble and a noise sounds from deep inside the rock.

AAAAAH…

It gets louder.

AAAAAAAAAH…

And louder.

AAAAAAAAAAAAAAH…

Until—

CHOOOOOOOOOOOOOOOOO!

Big Face Rock sneezes you out of its nostril like a speck of dust. You fly across Monkey Island, over the ocean and all the way back to the mainland, where you land in the middle of a crazy golf course.

Your mum is standing there, tapping her watch.

"About time," she says. "Now, see if you can hit

that ball into the windmill."

Go back to the start of the book to try again, or turn to page 21 to make a different choice.

You take out the rat and throw it at the little monkey ghost. She catches the critter, smiles widely and strokes it like a cat.

"You brought me a hamster!" she cries. "I've always wanted a hamster, but Mummy wouldn't let me get one."

"That mangy varmint ain't no hamster," says Jimmy Smallhands, before you can stop him. "That's a—"

"Gerbil!" you cut in. "It's a gerbil. It hasn't got fleas, it doesn't bite and it definitely does *not* smell of wee. You can keep it, if you want."

The little monkey ghost kisses the stinky rodent on the end of its twitchy nose. The rat seems to like her too.

"It's the best present *ever*," she says. "You can take the treasure. I don't need it anymore. It's just me and my new pet from now on," and she disappears through one of the walls.

"Wait!" you cry. "What treasure?"

"Upstairs," calls the ghost, from beyond the brickwork. "Near the window…"

76

At that moment, a tiny shadow falls over the empty room. It's Captain Fluffy-Beard and he's not alone – *his entire crew are with him!*

"So, it looks like you've found me hidin' place," snarls the monkey-pirate leader. "Think yer gunna steal me chocolate coins, do ye? We'll soon see about that, matey."

Crikey, talk about out of the cannon and into the shark-infested waters! Will you make a dash for the treasure, or get the heck out of here?

I'll take my crew outside to safety. No amount of chocolate is worth getting hurt for. Turn to page 25.

I'll make a dash for the staircase and reach the treasure before Captain Fluffy-Beard knows what's happening. Turn to page 61.

You walk west until a crumbling ruin appears in the distance.

There's a rotten window-frame over the doorway. It forms a perfect X at the top of the building, so you step inside and head for a dusty staircase in the back wall.

Your footsteps echo through the empty chamber.

"See?" you say to your crewmates. "It's fine in here. There are no such things as—"

One-Eyed Brenda points a trembling finger over your shoulder.

"Y-y-yargh," she breathes.

You turn to find a pale figure floating behind you. She's a monkey, but she's not a pirate. She's white all over, completely see-through and she looks really grumpy. Yikes! It's a little monkey ghost!

"What're you doing in my ruin?" demands the little monkey ghost. "Get out of here before I scare you away with my ghostly woo-ing."

GULP.

You'd really like to leave now, but you'd also like to search upstairs for the treasure. What are you going to do?

I'll jump for one of the creepers and climb away. Turn
to page 32.

Let's throw the rat at her. Turn to page 76.

You climb up to the crow's nest for a better look at the island. The view from here is fantastic. You can literally see right across to the other side of the—

SNAP!

Uh oh. The pole holding the crow's nest must have been damaged when the ship crashed and the extra weight has snapped it in two. You plummet towards the deck like a falling anchor, crash through the rotten wood and drop into the ship's galley.

You land next to a very hairy man.

He's carving a face into a coconut.

"How good of you to drop in on us," he says. "Oh dear, you seem to have hurt yourself. Have a drink out of Mr Coconut's head. It'll make you feel much better."

But drinking out of Mr Coconut's head doesn't make you feel better, so your crewmates wrap you up in bandages like an Egyptian mummy and send you back to the mainland to recover.

Go back to the start of the book to try again, or turn to page 54 to make a different choice.

You bite through the fishing-line and land on the grass at the side of the lagoon. Your crewmates take off like the wind, trying to escape the furry clutches of Big Baboon Bob.

But running is hard when you're dressed as a shark. You keep tripping over your tail and you can't see past your coconut teeth. Big Baboon Bob isn't the quickest monkey on the island, but he's catching up fast.

You'll need to think of a way to stop him, but how?

I'll ask Brenda to take out her telescopic eyeball and show it to Big Baboon Bob. That's enough to stop anyone in their tracks. Turn to page 5.

I'll shout, "Oh look, there's a bear!" and point over Big Baboon Bob's shoulder. Turn to page 60.

As you head towards the shipwreck on the eastern coast of the island, you pass a sign saying: WARNING – SHARK-INFESTED WATERS. It looks like you had a lucky escape when you avoided that lagoon, matey.

Swashbucklin'!

The land near the shipwreck is rocky and steep, and the huge wreckage of the old vessel looms on the coastline like the washed-up carcass of an ancient sea-monster. Two pieces of its great mast have snapped off and landed in an X shape on what's left of the decking. You'll need to take a closer look if you want to search for the treasure.

There are two ways to get up to the deck: you could climb the fallen rigging on the outside of the boat, or go in through a hole in its starboard side. Which would you like to do?

To climb the rigging on the outside of the shipwreck, turn to page 33.

To go through the hole and into the ship, turn to page 44.

You leave the water on the table and climb up a wooden flight of steps to the ship's deck. The old wreckage is creaky and damp, its sails are tattered and torn, the crow's nest has actual crows in it and the cannons are covered in barnacles.

You walk towards the broken mast to investigate the X. There's an old rum barrel directly below the cross, but you search inside it to find nothing more than seasnails and crabs. There's not a single chocolate coin on this whole bloomin' ship!

As you turn to leave, you see two identical monkey-pirates standing behind you. Eek! It's the Howler Twins! They're Captain Fluffy-Beard's first and second mates.

"What're ye doin' on our shipwreck, ye mangy varmint?" snarls the first twin.

"Yer a mangy varmint!" laughs the second. "Yo, ho, ho, ho, hooo!"

You try to think of a convincing answer, but instead you reply, "I'm delivering pizzas."

You're not sure why you said that.

"You can't deliver pizzas 'ere," says the first

Howler Twin. "It's only monkey-pirates what are allowed on Monkey Island, ye hornswagglin' barrel-bellied blighter."

"Yer a hornswagglin' barrel-bellied blighter!" laughs the second. "Yo, ho, ho, ho, hooo!"

"If ye ain't a monkey-pirate, you'll 'ave to walk the plank, ye filthy parrot-faced rapscallion."

"Yer a filthy parrot-faced rapscallion! Yo, ho, ho, ho, hooo!" The second twin lowers his furry eyebrows. "What's a pizza?"

How are you going to escape from the twins?

If you'd like to tell them you're a monkey-pirate, turn to page 47.

If you want to walk the plank and swim back to shore, turn to page 11.

You drop the rat and the little monkey ghost catches it. Her eyes sparkle as she strokes it like a cat.

"You brought me a hamster!" she cries. "I've always wanted a hamster, but my mummy wouldn't let me get one."

"That mangy varmint ain't no hamster," says Jimmy Smallhands, before you can stop him. "That's a—"

"Gerbil!" you cut in. "It's a gerbil. It hasn't got fleas, it doesn't bite and it definitely does *not* smell of wee. You can keep it, if you want."

The little monkey ghost kisses the stinky rodent on the end of its twitchy nose. The rat seems to like her too.

"It's the best present *ever!*" she cheers. "You can take the treasure. I don't need it anymore. It's just me and my new pet from now on," and she disappears through one of the walls.

"Wait!" you cry. "What treasure?"

"Upstairs," the ghost calls from beyond the brickwork. "Near the window…"

At that moment, a tiny shadow falls over the

empty room. It's Captain Fluffy-Beard and he's not alone – *his entire crew are with him!*

"So, it looks like you've found me hidin' place," snarls the monkey-pirate leader. "Think yer gunna steal me chocolate coins, do ye? We'll soon see about that, matey."

Crikey, talk about out of the cannon and into the shark-infested waters! Will you make a dash for the treasure, or get the heck out of here?

I'll take my crew outside to safety. Turn to page 25.

I'll make a dash for the staircase and reach the treasure before Captain Fluffy-Beard knows what's happening. Turn to page 30.

You march bravely onto the plank as if walking along a diving board at your local swimming pool and jump elegantly into the cool…

SPLODGE!

Oh, dear.

The tide is out at this time of day, so instead of landing in water, you've splatted into the muddy sand of the eastern coast. It takes five hours to dig yourself free, by which time the Howler Twins have captured your crewmates and eaten all of the chocolate coins for themselves.

Go back to the start of the book to try again, or turn to page 33 to make a different choice.

You run onto the quicksand to save One-Eyed Brenda, but the ground swallows you up like a tasty sandwich.

GULP!

You drop through the sand and find yourself in a secret underground tunnel. Brenda must have already wandered off and it's so dark down here you can't see where you're going, so you're forced to feel your way through the maze of passages.

It's three weeks before you find a way out. But you're an excellent friend for trying to rescue your crewmate, me hearty, so give yourself a piratey pat on the back then head to the mainland for a well-deserved rest.

Go back to the start of the book to try again, or turn to page 29 to make a different choice.

You climb down from the wreckage and onto the shore.

"Brenda," you say, "would you mind using your telescopic eyeball to search for another X?"

"Yargh!" replies One-Eyed Brenda.

A gentle whirring sound comes from inside the woman's head, as her eyeball spins in its socket.

WHIR! WHIR! WHIR! WHIR!

The pupil pops out like a tiny ice-cream cone.

POP!

And zooms in on the other side of the island with a rusty, *CREEEEEEEEAK!*

It's the most disgusting thing you've ever seen or heard in your life, but it's also pretty awesome.

Brenda points to the south of the island.

"She says there be another X on top o' Big Face Rock," explains Jimmy Smallhands. "But Big Face Rock is difficult to climb and dangerous too."

Brenda points to the west of the island.

"She also says there be an X in the window of an ancient ruin," says Jimmy, "but an evil spirit guards the buildin' and chases away anyone who goes near it.

I gotta tell ye, matey, I don't much fancy visitin' *either* place, but oi'll leave the choice up to ye."

Which X would you like to look at next?

An evil spirit? No, thanks! I'll go to Big Face Rock.

Turn to page 31.

An evil spirit? Cool! I'll go to the ancient ruin. Turn to page 78.

THE WRONG BUS

CHOOSE THE PAGE - UNLOCK THE ADVENTURE

A STORYQUEST BOOK BY
BECCI MURRAY

The Wrong Bus

A STORYQUEST BOOK BY

BECCI MURRAY

For Jessie

STORYQUEST
CHOOSE THE PAGE - UNLOCK THE ADVENTURE

ISBN: 978-1-9162069-8-4

Published by Llama House Children's Books

Welcome to your StoryQuest challenge, the book where YOU are in charge of what happens and YOU are the star of the adventure.

Start your quest on the first page, where your challenge will be explained. At the end of each chapter you'll find two options – choose a page to decide what you want to do next.

As a bonus feature, every StoryQuest book has a SPECIAL CHARACTER hidden amongst the pages. Find the character, and they'll give you a STORYQUEST STAR. This will help you unlock the ultimate ending to your adventure.

There are SO many different paths and SO many different endings – some are good, some are bad, some are happy, some are sad. Which will you choose? Will you complete the challenge? And where will your story end?

Good luck, intrepid StoryQuester, and happy reading!

Waiting for a bus is more boring than anything else in the whole, entire universe.

Your mum's rabbiting on about something she saw on the telly (yawn), there's a man in a suit reading a newspaper (double-yawn) and old Mrs Pollychamp from next door is fiddling with her false teeth (triple-yawn), when suddenly the sky opens up and an enormous red bus bursts through the clouds.

VROOSH!

Four bright lights beam down from the bus's wheels as it lands on the road in front of you. With a hiss, the doors open and a robot walks out. She has legs like drainpipes, arms like springs and a face like a wok.

"Greetings, humanoids," she bleeps. "I am a Bio-Robotic Intelligent Android Navigator from Space Zone 12, but you can call me BRIAN."

"Hello, BRIAN," you reply, as your mum's face turns grey. "What brings you to planet Earth?"

"I am the driver of this intergalactic school bus, but my spacecraft has been hit by a meteor and my memory box has been damaged." The robot points to a dent in her forehead. "I have forgotten almost forty-four billion gigabytes of data."

"Oh, dear," you reply. "That looks painful. Does it

hurt?"

"Young humanoid," the robot replies, "that is like asking a tin of baked-beans if it has the tummy ache, but you can call me BRIAN." The robot scratches her head. "Did I already say that?"

"Yes, you did. Can you remember anything at all, BRIAN?"

"Well, I remember collecting these children from Miss Tentacle's School for Every Alien," she says, "and I remember it is my job to return each child safely back to their parents."

You look up through the windows of the bus. A group of alien children stares back at you. Some have flippers, some are covered in hair, some have mouths like bananas and some are asleep in the luggage rack.

"The problem is," the robot continues, "I cannot remember where their home planets are located, so I have landed here on Earth to ask for assistance." She pauses, and then, "Young humanoid, will you fly this space-bus and navigate the deepest, darkest depths of the endless universe to save these children?"

"*Me?!*" you gasp. "But I can't fly a bus!"

"Flying a bus is easy," she says, "but navigating the cosmos can sometimes prove tricky. Which is why I have some useful items to aid your success."

The robot reaches an extendable arm back into the

bus and pulls a plastic tub from under the driver's seat. You don't know what you were hoping she'd pull out from under that seat, but a packed-lunch definitely wasn't it.

"Are those…sandwiches?" you ask.

"Affirmative," grins the robot, meaning 'yes.' "Moon cheese and starfruit chutney. My favourites. Sandwiches are essential for every outer-space journey."

She points to a silver handle on the dashboard of the bus.

"We also have this rocket boost lever. With one pull, our bus will hurtle across the universe at the speed of light."

"That sounds…terrifying," you say.

"And thirdly, you have me, BRIAN, the most advanced satellite navigation robot this side of the Lunar Peninsular." You eye the big dent in BRIAN's forehead and smile politely. "So, young humanoid, will you help a broken satnav robot return these alien children to their home planets?"

A buzz of excitement zips up your spine like a bright shooting star.

"Okay," you reply, "let's do it!"

Mum's eyes bulge like a couple of ping-pong balls as BRIAN grabs you by the jumper, lifts you onto the bus and plonks you down in the driver's seat.

"That is most excellent news," bleeps the robot. "I shall return you to your mother when our quest is complete. But remember, you must locate the *correct planets* for each group of children or we shall all be lost in space forever," and with the push of a button, your space-bus soars up through the cloudy skies of planet Earth and into the endless universe.

Your StoryQuest has begun! Turn to page 142 to start your adventure.

"I'm sorry, officer," you reply. "I didn't realise I needed a license to fly this bus."

"Don't worry," the alien replies, "if you don't have a license, you can take a test. It won't take long – in fact, there's only one question." The officer takes a pamphlet out of his pocket and opens it up. "Ah, yes, here it is: which button will activate the windscreen wipers of your space-vehicle?"

Zoinks! This is the quickest driver's test *ever!* But you didn't know the bus even *had* windscreen wipers!

"If you press the correct button," the officer goes on, "I'll give you your license. But press the wrong button, and your bus will be confiscated and you'll have to catch the next space-train out of here."

There are only two buttons to choose from. One is orange and the other is pink. Which button will you press?

To press the orange button, turn to page 186.
To press the pink button, turn to page 133.

"BRIAN might be a bit dented," you tell the man in the dressing gown, "and she's forgotten forty-four billion gigabytes of data, but she's my friend and she's helping me finish this quest. I don't want to swap her."

The golden android sniffs and an oily tear runs down his face.

"Do you see that, Master Jake?" he chokes. "*That* is true loyalty. You could learn a thing or two from this young human."

"Hm," says the man in the dressing gown, "but tell me, kid, if your satnav robot's broken, how are you navigating your way through space?"

"I'm just guessing really," you tell him, "and sometimes I ask people for directions. Hey, I don't suppose you know where Sweatiolis is, do you?"

"Kid," he replies, "I've been flying this ship since 1977 – of course I know the way to Sweatiolis. All you have to do is head for the Triangular Sun and it'll be right there in front of you. I went there once with my father. Strange man. Kind of grumpy."

You thank Master Jake for his help, then the green alien shows you back to your bus and you take to the skies once again.

In the near-distance, a Triangular Sun twinkles

like a sparkly wedge of cheese. The air on the bus grows hotter as you travel towards it and you feel like a piece of corn in a microwave, about to go pop at any moment, when suddenly you notice a slivery planet orbiting the sun's highest point. It's Sweatiolis – cosmic!

Sweatiolis has fifteen yellow moons and a small space-rock hovering close to your bus. An old alien is sat on a deckchair, holding a big, red button. Her bottom is as wide as the rock and she looks like a giant potato, only more knobbly and without the mud.

"Who's that?" you whisper to BRIAN.

"She looks like a toll collector," the robot explains. "Sweatiolis has a silver forcefield protecting it. That alien will not open the barrier unless we pay her a fee."

As BRIAN searches her disc-drive for loose change, you pull up next to the rock and open the window. The toll collector grimaces through the gap as she holds out her hand. You don't have any money and it doesn't look like BRIAN does either. What are you going to do?

☆

I'll give her a sandwich from the lunchbox. Turn to page 171.

I'll talk nicely to her and explain what's happened. Turn to page 117.

Turning the bus with lightning speed, you slam your foot on the accelerator.

VROOSH!

Your spacecraft zooms away from the avalanche and along the pear-slice road, where a mango-car suddenly pulls out of a side-street. At the last moment, you stamp on the brake and screech to a halt, where you turn to see the enormous grapes moving closer by the second.

You watch as they tumble down Kiwi Mountain, past the Banana Forest and along the pear-slice road, until one by one they slam into the side of your bus.

SPLAT! SPLAT! SPLAT! SPLAT! SPLAT! SPLAT!

The fruits explode like purple pimples, burying your bus in a sticky mess. It'll take forever to dig your way out of here.

"Perhaps we should call Miss Tentacle," suggests BRIAN. "She has family here on Fruitopia who may help us out of our sticky situation."

Hurriedly, you press the hologramophone button. Miss Tentacle appears in the aisle of the bus. She's making a noise like a sheep playing a harmonica.

"MAA-AA-AA-AA-AA-AA-AA-AA—"

When she realises you can see (and hear) her, she

stops.

"Oh, hello," she says. "I was just practising my operatic scales."

Crikey, she was *singing!*

You thought someone had stood on her tentacle.

When you explain what happened, Miss Tentacle looks out of the window. She sees the alien driver get out of his mango-car. He has four purple tentacles, a long trunk and a candyfloss beard. In a funny sort of way, he looks like an upside-down version of the headmistress.

"Well, bless my stars and moons!" Miss Tentacle exclaims. "It's my twin brother, *Mr* Tentacle. You've saved him from a grape avalanche, you wonderful human! I'll get him to call a few friends and dig you out of that mess. Keep up the good work though – you're doing a great job. Now, where did I put my tuning fork…?"

Before long, a hundred Fruitopians are digging you out of the goo and waving you off as you leave the planet Fruitopia. The blackhole is still swirling like an astronomical washing machine as you pass by, so you steer carefully around it as BRIAN pushes the satnav button on her arm.

"The fourth bus-stop we must find is on a planet called Noctron," says the robot. "To locate the planet

Noctron, we must bear left – *BLEEP!* Bear left – *BLEEP!* Bear left – *BLEEP!* Bear left – *BLEEP!*"

That's strange. This is the first time BRIAN has only given you one direction to follow, but turning left will send you into the blackhole.

"I'm not sure that's a good idea," you tell her. "Perhaps we should bear right instead."

"No!" cries the robot. "Bear left! Bear left!" She points into the blackhole. "Young humanoid, there is a *bear* on our left!"

Confused, you look out of the window. Well, blow me down with a solar wind, there really *is* a bear on your left! It's a huge bear made completely of stars, running through space like it's out for a stroll in the park.

The bear beckons you into the blackhole with his twinkly paw. Do you want to follow him?

A space-bear? Cool! Let's follow him! Turn to page 146.

A space-bear? Eek! Let's get out of here! Turn to page 125.

You activate the inflatable tyre mechanism and the wheels of your bus swell-up like four huge rubber-rings. They push against the windows like mutant slugs as the air inside them lifts your spacecraft slowly up to the surface of the ocean.

The bus bobs on the shimmering waves as you open the doors with a hiss. Five silvery children dive into the water, as their parents' heads break the surface.

You've taken the first group of children back to their home planet!

"Excellent work, young humanoid," congratulates BRIAN. "Shall we now move on to our next planet?" She presses the satnav button on her arm. "The second bus-stop we must find is on a planet called Sweatiolis. To locate the planet Sweatiolis, we must travel towards the Triangular Sun – *BLEEP!* We must chase the shooting star - *BLEEP!* Travel towards the Triangular Sun - *BLEEP!* Chase the shooting star – *BLEEP!*"

I'll travel towards the Triangular Sun please. Turn to page 155.

I'd like to follow the shooting star. Turn to page 140.

You carry on in the hope you have enough fuel, but your spacecraft sounds more like a steam train than a bus.

CHUG…CHUG…CHUG…CHUG…

It's jumping from star to star like a kangaroo on a pogo-stick, stuttering over planets and spluttering past moons, until suddenly, with one final cough, the engine stops.

You've run out of fuel. Your space-bus has broken down and you're floating around in the nothingness with no power. Even the hologramophone won't work, so you wait patiently until Miss Tentacle notices your lateness and sends a tow-ship out to rescue you.

Go back to the start of the book to try again, or turn to page 126 to make a different choice.

As you fly towards the brilliant white light, you realise it's not a planet, it's a nebular star.

Nebular stars are awesome! There's so much gravity on a nebular star, it acts like a super-strength magnet. Space-junk from across the universe is sucked in and stretched out like pizza dough, until it ends up like a long strand of spaghetti.

Sadly, this also means being on a bus near a nebular star is a really bad idea. The light pulls you in at half the speed of light and stretches you out like a piece of elastic.

You can't steer a bus with noodle-arms so your quest is over. But all this talk of spaghetti has made you hungry, so you order an intergalactic food delivery and feast on spaghettified spaghetti until Miss Tentacle hears about your predicament and sends you straight back to Earth.

Go back to the start of the book to try again, or turn to page 157 to make a different choice.

When you open the window, a terrible stink fills the bus. It smells worse than a cabbage-eating skunk in a sewer.

"Phooey!" you cry, pinching your nose. "What's that horrible smell?"

"I believe the pong you're referring to comes from the fifteen moons of Sweatiolis," says BRIAN. "They are made out of cheese and are well-known for their astronomical whiff."

The stinky air makes your head dizzy and your vision blurred. You can't see to drive, so BRIAN presses the hologramophone button and the headmistress appears in the aisle of the bus, snoring like an elephant with a trumpet stuck up its nostril.

"ZZZZZ! ZZZZZ! ZZZZ- Oh, erm, hello," she splutters. "I was just resting my eyes." She wasn't. She was snoring like an elephant. "How can I help you?"

"Miss Tentacle, I am afraid the young humanoid has opened a window near the fifteen moons of Sweatiolis," explains BRIAN, "and the terrible whiff of cheese has overpowered their senses."

"That's awful news," says Miss Tentacle. "We must take the young human back to an Earthean doctor as soon as possible. Wait there, BRIAN – I'll send someone out to fetch you."

A tow-ship arrives. It pulls you back to your home planet, where the doctor says you'll be fine but the smell lingers on you for weeks and everyone at school thinks you stepped in something a dog did.

Go back to the start of the book to try again, or turn to page 131 to make a different choice.

"I'm not falling for that one," you tell the impish aliens, "you're making it up. Come on, get off the bus without a donut and let's see if you really *are* arrested by the Donut Police."

You usher the banana-mouthed children through the doorway and watch as they scamper away from the bus. They're heading straight for the hatch of the Blue Moon Donut Café.

"I cannot see the Donut Police," says BRIAN, with confusion, "and I cannot see the bus-stop either. I fear those alien children have been telling us lies, young humanoid – and I believe we are on the wrong planet."

Drat those pesky aliens!

What are you going to do?

I'd like to call Miss Tentacle on the hologramophone.
Turn to page 159.
I'll tell the children to get back on the bus. Turn to page 169.

You decide to talk nicely to the toll collector and explain what happened.

"Hello," you say. "How are you?"

The alien smiles.

Actually, it could be a snarl.

Whatever it is, it looks like it hurts.

"Nrgh," growls the toll collector.

"I, erm, really like your clothes," you go on. "They're very—"

But then you realise she's a talking potato and she's not wearing any clothes. Awkward.

The toll collector pushes her hand closer towards you.

"You gotta pay," she says, "so gimme your money or *CLEAR OFF!*"

The force of her voice ruffles your hair and a drop of alien spit lands on your face.

"The thing is," you say, wiping it off with the back of your hand, "I'm on a quest to save these children, but I don't have any money. Please can you press the button and let me through without paying? Just this once?"

The toll collector curls her rubbery lips up under her nose and looks carefully into your eyes. Then she

shoves the forcefield button into her mouth and crunches it up like a boiled sweet.

CHOMP! CHOMP! CHOMP!

You take that as a 'no.'

The forcefield won't be opening any time soon, not now the button is inside the toll collector's belly, so you can't get to Sweatiolis to return the second group of children. Never mind, StoryQuester – why not go back and see if the toll collector would like a nice sandwich instead?

Go back to the start of the book to try again, or turn to page 106 to make a different choice.

The golden comet leads you to a blue planet with a rippling surface. An immense ring circles around it, glittering in the light of a small, white sun. It reminds you of Saturn, but either you're seeing things or...*that ring has teeth!*

"Young humanoid," says BRIAN, "there is a giant space-eel guarding this planet. Space-eels are very rare and very dangerous. It will make entering the atmosphere quite tricky."

Okay, StoryQuester, how will you reach the planet without being eaten by the evil space-fish?

I'll fly quickly and take the space-eel by surprise. Turn to page 174.

I'll approach the eel slowly then swerve at the last second. Turn to page 199.

As you dock into the fuel space station, a pink alien scurries over to fill up your tank.

"I should warn you," she chatters, unscrewing the cap, "putting the wrong type of fuel in a spacecraft can permanently damage the engine. You'd better hope this is your lucky day." She taps on the bonnet of your bus. "All done. I'll send the bill to Miss Tentacle. Okay, then – give it a try."

A shooting-star sweeps overhead as you press the ignition button. You close your eyes, make a wish and…

VROOSH!

The new fuel turns out to be even *better* than the old fuel – huzzah! – so you leave the fuel station and head-off in search of Miss Tentacle's School for Every Alien.

"The school is in Space Zone 12," says BRIAN, "and no bump on the head will make me forget where my own galaxy is located – this way, StoryQuester!"

The satnav robot directs you across the starry plains, past the Lunar Peninsular and onto Space Zone 12, where a deep crimson planet looms up through a misty sky. There are five moons spinning madly around it, like a Ferris wheel stuck on high-speed.

Gah! Just when you think your quest is complete, the universe throws a handful of hypersonic moons at you. This is going to take some skilful driving.

What's your final move, StoryQuester?

I'll pull the rocket boost lever. Turn to page 151.

I'll let BRIAN steer us through. Turn to page 166.

"Not to worry," smiles Miss Tentacle, "you've taken all the children back to their home planets and proved you are the best intergalactic bus driver this side of the Lunar Peninsular – and frankly, I've had enough stars to last me a lifetime anyway."

The headmistress takes out a remote control and presses one of the buttons. A small bubble-like spacecraft zooms out from behind the school building and stops in front of you.

"What's that?" you gasp.

"A space-pod," Miss Tentacle replies. "*Your* space-pod, to be precise. It's a little thank you gift for all your hard work."

Your very own spacecraft – cosmic!

BRIAN opens the hatch and signals for you to climb in.

"This space-pod has been fitted with a built-in satellite navigation system," smiles the robot, "so you will have no difficulty in finding your way back to Earth. Safe journey home, young humanoid, and many thanks for your assistance."

You wave goodbye to BRIAN and Miss Tentacle, then you take to the skies of Space Zone 12 in your new space-pod, where you travel back through the endless universe until planet Earth appears in the distance.

You land at your usual bus-stop. Your mum's still standing there, her mouth's still hanging open and her face is still grey. She hasn't moved since you left.

"Do you like my new spaceship?" you ask her. "Miss Tentacle gave it to me. Where shall we go first, Mum? Aquavon, Sweatiolis, Fruitopia, Noctron? Or we could just go to Mars, if you like," and as your mum's face turns greyer than a cloudy day on the dark side of Noctron, you realise waiting at a bus-stop isn't quite so boring after all.

Congratulations! You've completed your quest and now you're the owner of a brand-new space-pod!

If you want to find the StoryQuest Star, go back to the start of the book and try your adventure again. Or take a look in the back of this book for more choose-the-page StoryQuest adventures.

You order a donut for each of the five blackcurrant-eyed aliens and before BRIAN can find her wallet to pay for them, the alien children munch them down in one bite.

CHOMP!

"Hey!" you cry. "You said the Donut Police would arrest you for going outside without a donut, so why have you eaten them?"

The aliens giggle. They've told you a lie. They don't live on this planet. They're from a place called Fruitopia and feeding donuts to a Fruitopian is like giving candyfloss to a rabbit. The sugary food stirs up their tummies like soup in a blender until—

"BLARRRRRGH!"

They're sick all over the back seat of the bus.

You'll have to take them to space-hospital for a nice dose of prune juice to sooth their grumbly tummies, so you can't carry on with your quest. But don't worry, StoryQuester, you can try again once you've cleaned up the mess.

Go back to the start of the book to try again, or turn to page 150 to make a different choice.

Blackholes are even scarier than space-eels, so there's no way you're following that bear. You watch as the starry bear vanishes into the swirling darkness and wonder what will become of the poor creature.

BRIAN presses the satnav button on her arm.

"Our final bus-stop," she repeats, "can be found on the planet Noctron. To locate the planet Noctron, we must travel towards the purple nebular – *BLEEP!* We should chase the flaming meteor – *BLEEP!* Travel towards the purple nebular – *BLEEP!* Chase the flaming meteor – *BLEEP!*"

The purple nebular is beautiful – let's go there. Turn to page 157.

The flaming meteor looks more exciting – let's chase it. Turn to page 154.

ZZZ-POP!

Miss Tentacle is taking a selfie as she appears in the aisle of the bus. When she realises you can see her, she stops pouting and holds out her phone to show you the photograph.

"Does my trunk look big in this?" she asks.

It does.

Her trunk would look big on a mammoth.

"Erm, no," you answer, "not at all, Miss Tentacle. Sorry to disturb you, but we've landed on the light side of Noctron and the children won't wake up. I'm worried they might be ill."

"They're not ill," replies the headmistress, "they're nocturnal. The Noctrons live on the dark side of their planet – they won't wake up in broad daylight. They wear sunglasses to stay awake at school, so whatever you do, don't let them go outside in the daylight or they'll go to sleep for a week."

The headmistress pauses to admire herself on the screen of her phone, and then, "By the way," she adds, "congratulations on finding your last planet. Return the bus to my school once you've located the bus-stop on the dark side of Noctron and your quest will be over. Now, where did I put my selfie-stick…?" and with a faint crackle, the hologram fades.

With no time to lose, you steer your spacecraft into the thick blackness of the dark side, where the children of Noctron stir in their sleep. A hologram of a bus flickers and a group of bat-like parents wave as their nocturnal children fly into the night.

Do you know what this means, StoryQuester? It means you've taken *all* of the children safely back to their home planets and are officially the most spectacular space navigator in the history of the cosmos!

All you have to do now is take the bus back to—

BEEP! BEEP! BEEP! BEEP! BEEP!

Take the bus back to Miss Tentacle and your quest will be—

BEEP! BEEP! BEEP! BEEP! BEEP!

And your quest will be—

BEEP! BEEP! BEEP! BEEP! BEEP!

Your quest will—

BEEP! BEEP! BEEP! BEEP! BEEP!

What in Jupiter's name is that awful beeping noise?

A red light illuminates on the dashboard. Your fuel tank is almost empty and you might not have enough power to fly back to Miss Tentacle's School for Every Alien without filling-up.

"There is a space fuel station not far from here,"

notes BRIAN, with a press of her satnav button. "But it sells a different type of fuel to the one we use in this bus. There is a chance it will work. But there is also a chance the new fuel will cause our bus to evaporate into a gazzilion tiny droplets of molten metal."

Blimey.

Well, this is quite a pickle. Will you risk filling-up with the new fuel, or see if you can make it back to school without it?

I'll carry on without filling up. Turn to page 112.
I'd like to go to the fuel station please. Turn to page 120.

Dodging the shooty-beam-beams is harder than you thought. Whoever's firing them is really good at it. They're hitting your bus with every shot.

But here's the thing about shooty-beam-beams. All they are is little green lights that go *PYOW-PYOW-PYOW!* They can't hurt you, so you steer your bus safely away from the gigantic spaceship until it's nothing more than a tiny speck of grey in the distance.

Marvellous!

"It looks like the shooting star we were following has gone," you say to BRIAN, searching the black sky. "But, look, there's the Triangular Sun. Perhaps we could go that way instead."

"A most excellent idea," the robot replies. "The Triangular Sun is a very interesting phenomenon, young humanoid. All of the sun's heat is funnelled out of its topmost tip, making it the hottest place in the entire cosmos."

Orbiting the tip of the Triangular Sun is a silvery planet surrounded by fifteen yellow moons. When you fly towards it, you come to a small floating space-rock. It's no bigger than a boulder and there's an old alien sat on it in a deckchair. She looks like a potato, she's holding a big red button and she's wearing a badge that says, Welcome to Sweatiolis.

You've found your next planet – cosmic!

"Who's that?" you ask BRIAN.

"She is a toll collector," the robot replies. "Sweatiolis has a silver-forcefield around it to keep out any unwanted visitors. That alien will not open the barrier unless we pay her a fee of 10 space dollars each."

As BRIAN checks her disc-drives for spare change, you pull up next to the rock and open the doors. The toll collector grimaces through the doorway, then she holds her hand out for your payment.

You don't have any money and it looks like BRIAN has forgotten where she put her wallet. How will you get past the potatoey alien?

I'll give her a sandwich from BRIAN's lunchbox instead of the cash. Turn to page 171.

I'll talk nicely to the toll collector and explain what's happened – she might let us through without paying. Turn to page 201.

Thinking fast, you pull the lunchbox out from under your seat and offer the toll collector a sandwich. The potatoey woman squints at it through narrowed eyes.

"Is that a sandwich?" she frowns.

"Of course it is not a sandwich," says BRIAN. "It is a cake."

That's strange. Why is your satnav robot lying about a sandwich?

"In that case," says the toll collector, "I suppose I could manage one little bite. You'll still have to pay a fee though – nobody goes through the forcefield without paying a fee."

The alien's mouth starts to salivate. Then she helps herself to one of the sandwiches, takes a bite and…

POOF!

…vanishes in a flash of blinding light.

You stare in horror at the empty deckchair.

"What did we do to her?!" you cry. "Where did she go?! And why did you tell her that sandwich was a cake?!"

"If the toll collector had known it was a sandwich, young humanoid, she would not have eaten it," replies BRIAN. "Sandwiches have special teleportation

131

powers in space – that tasty snack has transported the toll collector to the other side of this galaxy, where she can no longer charge us a fee to land on this planet."

Awesome!

Something red catches your eye from the seat of the toll collector's deckchair – it's the forcefield button! You reach out, take hold of the object and press. The silvery exterior of the planet opens up like an elevator door as the forcefield unlocks.

Double awesome!

But as Sweatiolis emerges from beneath it like a big, rusty ball-bearing, the heat of the Triangular Sun becomes almost unbearable. You'll have to cool down the air inside the bus if you want to land, otherwise you'll be roasted to a crisp.

Triple awe—

No, wait. That's not awesome at all.

What are you going to do?

To turn on the air-conditioning, turn to page 191.
To open the windows and create a breeze, turn to page 114.

You press the pink button and…

KA-BOOF!

…you activate the ejector seat.

Oops.

In the blink of an eye, a hatch in the roof opens up as the driver's chair hurls you out of the bus, where you drift through space like a stringless balloon, unsure whether you're falling *down* or floating *up*, until you enter the atmosphere of a nearby planet.

At this point, there's no question about which direction you're travelling – you're definitely falling down. But luckily the ground on this planet is soft, so it's a bit like landing on a giant marshmallow. What's more, the creatures who live here are kind aliens who love nothing more than making friends with creatures from other planets. They smother you with big, slobbery, alien kisses and accept you into their world as one of their own, where you live for three years until being discovered by a passing astronaut.

Go back to the start of the book to try again, or turn to page 105 to make a different choice.

You carry on, hoping you have enough fuel to reach Miss Tentacle's school, but your spacecraft sounds more like a steam-train than a bus.

CHUG, CHUG, CHUG, CHUG, CHUG…

What's more, it's jumping from star to star like a kangaroo on a pogo-stick, hopping over planets and leaping past comets, until suddenly, with one final splutter, the engine stops.

CH-CH-CH-CH-CH…CHUG.

You've ran out of fuel. Your space-bus has broken down in the middle of space and you're floating around in the nothingness with no power whatsoever. Even the hologramophone won't work without fuel, so you're forced to sit patiently until Miss Tentacle notices your lateness and sends out a tow-ship to find you.

Go back to the start of the book to try again, or turn to page 193 to make a different choice.

You've been wanting to try the rocket booster for *ages*, so you carefully take hold of the lever and pull.

Nothing happens.

"Why aren't we moving?" you ask BRIAN.

"Our exhaust pipe is blocked," the robot replies, as your bus starts shaking like a jelly on a train. "Those naughty young aliens have put something in there and the rocket booster is building up inside our engine. It will come out eventually, young humanoid, but the boost may be much bigger than we—"

KABOOM!

The size of the blast takes you by surprise. Your hands slip from the steering wheel as the bus rockets forwards. It crashes into the side of Kiwi Mountain with a loud splat, dislodging a bunch of oversized grapes that were balanced on top of its peak like purple boulders. The giant fruits thunder downhill towards your bus. Grape avalanche! Argh! Quick, get out of the way!

I'm facing the wrong direction – let's turn this bus around! Turn to page 108.

There's no time for that – I'll reverse us all out of here! Turn to page 137.

On the light side of the planet, there's a sign saying:

Welcome to Noctron

You've reached your final destination – cosmic!

The planet Noctron looks similar to Earth, but there are no buildings, no streets and no signs of life. There certainly aren't any bus-stops.

What's more, the children who live here are still asleep in the luggage rack. They've been snoring the whole journey. Do you think they're okay?

I think they're fine. Let's wake them up and tell them they're home. Turn to page 162.

I'll check with Miss Tentacle. Turn to page 126.

You put the bus into reverse, stamp your foot on the pedal and…

VROOSH!

Your spacecraft rushes backwards, away from Kiwi Mountain, away from the grape avalanche and onto the pear-slice road.

But it's hard to see where you're going when you're travelling in reverse and suddenly…

BOOF!

Your bus ploughs into a mango-car and you come to a standstill in the middle of the road. A fountain of fruit juice squirts out from the car's bonnet. The driver looks angry. In fact, he looks furious. He gets out, shakes a tentacle at you, then starts pummelling your spacecraft with pomegranate pips as the grape avalanche continues to roll down the pear-slice road.

One by one the enormous fruits slam into the side of your bus.

SPLAT!

SPLAT!

SPLAT!

SPLAT!

They explode like big, purple pimples, burying your spacecraft in a sticky mess. It'll take forever to dig your way out of here.

"We should call Miss Tentacle," suggests BRIAN. "She has family here on Fruitopia who may help us out of our sticky situation."

When you press the hologramophone button. Miss Tentacle appears in the aisle of the bus. She's making a noise like a goat with a broken trumpet.

"*MAA-AA-AA-AA-AA-AA-AA-AA —*"

Realising you can see (and hear) her, she stops.

"Oh, hello," she says. "I was just practising my operatic scales."

Crikey, she was *singing!*

You thought she'd caught her trunk in a car-door.

Hurriedly, you explain what happened and Miss Tentacle looks out of the window. She sees the alien driver throwing pomegranate seeds at your bus. He has four purple tentacles, a long trunk and a candyfloss beard. In a funny sort of way, he looks like an upside-down version of Miss Tentacle.

"That's my brother!" cries the headmistress. "That's *Mr* Tentacle!"

She glowers at you through her moon-shaped spectacles.

"Humanoid," she snarls, "I'm sending a tow-ship to pull you out of there, then you'd better start saving your pocket money – you owe my brother a new mango-car," and as the hologram flickers out, your StoryQuest comes to a very sticky end.

Go back to the start of the book to try again, or turn to page 135 to make a different choice.

The shooting star slides across the darkness like a lone firework, its golden tail glittering in the murky sky.

Quietly, you close your eyes and make a wish.

"I wish for the most epic space adventure the universe has ever known," you whisper.

As the words leave your lips, a disc-shaped spaceship swoops in from behind a distant moon. It's at least a thousand times bigger than your own spacecraft and it looks like a huge dinner plate (only fancier and with more lights).

A large window looks into the cockpit. You see a golden android sitting next to a yeti and a woman with two currant buns stuck to the sides of her head. A man in a dressing gown stands up. He sees your bus, pulls out a giant glow-stick and waves it around like a sword.

Could this be the start of the most epic space adventure the universe has ever known?

Suddenly, and without warning, a string of green lights sprays out of the spaceship like confetti.

PYOW! PYOW! PYOW! PYOW! PYOW!

"Young humanoid, the spaceship is attacking us with its shooty-beam-beams," says BRIAN. "We must do something before our bus is blasted to smithereens."

Quick, StoryQuester, do something and fast!

The shooty-beam-beams look harmless – let's land on the spaceship and say hello. Turn to page 163.
The shooty-beam-beams look dangerous – let's dodge them and get the heck out of here. Turn to page 129.

You soar through the dazzling starlit sky in your space-bus, circling planets and speeding past moons as if carried along on the wings of butterflies (really strong butterflies with big muscles), when suddenly…

ZZZ-POP!

A purple alien materialises next to you.

Yikes! Where did *she* come from?

The alien has six tentacles, pink candyfloss hair and a pair of moon-shaped spectacles perched on the end of her trunk. She peers over her glasses to inspect you like a hair she just found in her sandwich.

"BRIAN," she croaks, her voice sounding a bit like a creaky door, "why is there a *human* driving my space-bus?"

"Greetings, Miss Tentacle," the robot replies. Crikey, it's the headmistress of Miss Tentacle's School for Every Alien! "My memory was damaged in a meteor crash, so this young humanoid is taking the children back to their home planets."

The headmistress sniffs at you with her long, holographic trunk and her face flickers.

"Hmm," she breathes, "I suppose your enthusiasm is to be admired. Very well, human, I will trust you to look after these children and am most grateful for your help."

"You're welcome, Miss Tentacle," you reply.

"If you need my assistance," the headmistress goes on, "you may call me on the hologramophone. I'll help if I can, but if I have to send out a tow-ship to rescue you, your quest will be over. Now, if you'll excuse me, I have a very busy day ahead," and with a crackle, the headmistress is gone.

BRIAN presses the satnav button at the top of her arm – your journey is about to begin!

"The first bus-stop we must find is on a planet called Aquavon," says the robot. Her satnav voice sounds like the woman who reads the news on TV. "To locate the planet Aquavon we must head for the giant star-cluster – *BLEEP!* We should follow the golden comet – *BLEEP!* Head for the giant star-cluster – *BLEEP!* Follow the golden comet – *BLEEP!*"

BRIAN is the most advanced satnav robot this side of Space Zone 12, but she also has a big dent in her forehead. Your robot's not sure which way you should travel. Which one of her instructions will you follow?

To head for the giant star-cluster, turn to page 195.

To follow the golden comet, turn to page 119.

A stream of stars disappears into the swirling darkness of the blackhole as you fly towards it. The hole pulls at your spacecraft, trying to suck you into its murky depths like a fly down a plughole, but you keep your distance and eventually pass by unharmed.

Beyond the blackhole, there's an orange. That's right – an orange. An *actual* orange, only the size of a planet. There's even an apple-moon orbiting its stem.

With no toll collectors or space-eels blocking your path, you enter the planet's atmosphere and find yourself in a world made entirely of fruit.

It's quite a sight and it smells delicious. The trees have bananas for trunks, the houses are made out of coconuts, the mountains are kiwis and the pavements are lined with slices of pear. And there, next to the cherry-juice river, is a holographic bus-stop.

You've found the planet Fruitopia – cosmic!

With a squelch, you land on the sticky ground. The five alien children with furry green skin bounce to the front of the bus. They jump through the open doorway, run past their parents and disappear around the back of the bus.

"Okay, BRIAN," you say, "only one planet left – let's get on with our quest."

You press the ignition button to start the engine.
CHUG, CHUG, CHUG, CHUG...

But the bus won't start.

"The children of Fruitopia are well-known for making mischief," says BRIAN. "I fear they have played a trick on us by somehow disabling our spacecraft."

Oo, the little scallywags!

What will you do, StoryQuester?

I'll get out and see if I can fix it. Turn to page 176.
Let's pull the rocket booster lever – that should get the engine started. Turn to page 135.

Being inside a blackhole is strangely unreal. Your bus drifts through an obstacle course of curious objects (a hat stand, a cement mixer, an old cruise ship, a piano, even the Statue of Liberty), all bent out of shape by the pull of the blackhole. And amongst the chaos, a big sparkly bear waves hello as he surfs through the swirling darkness on the back of an old ironing-board.

Suddenly, a starry man leaps out from behind a giant food-blender.

"Aha!" he shouts. "At last, I have you, bear! Prepare to meet thy doom as I thwart you with my mighty sword!"

The man swings a starry weapon and the bear freezes. The poor creature looks terrified.

"Excuse me," you call out of your window, "has that bear done something wrong? Only, I think you're frightening him."

The man turns his gigantic head to peer through the windscreen of your spacecraft. His eyeball alone is the size of your bus. It's as if a whole galaxy is alive in his face.

"Listen, oh small and insignificant human," says the man, "two thousand years ago, that bear stole my belt. And what's the good of a famous huntsman if his

146

trousers keep falling down?"

"You're a famous huntsman?" you frown.

The man pulls a face like you just passed wind.

"Yes," he says. "Don't you recognise me? I'm the mighty Orion, hero of Greek mythology, son of Poseidon, eternal hunter of the skies. You must've seen me in a film or something?"

"I don't think so," you reply, "and I don't want to upset you, but I'm not sure you *are* the son of Poseidon – I think you're a constellation."

"HOW DARE YOU INSULT THE MIGHTY ORION?!" The universe shudders at the sound of Orion's voice, and then, "What's a constellation?" he adds.

"It's a pattern of stars," you explain. "Sometimes the stars make up the shape of an animal, or an object, or, well, a huntsman."

Orion looks himself up and down.

"In that case, you might be right." He shrugs. "But I'm still going to thwart this bear with my mighty sword."

The petrified animal cowers behind a passing marshmallow, his paws in front of his eyes. You can't let the huntsman thwart the poor creature, even if he *has* stolen his belt.

"Please don't hurt him," you say. "If he's taken

something of yours, why don't you just ask for it back?"

Orion thinks about this for a moment.

"Eternal huntsmen don't *ask* for things," he says, "they thwart people with their mighty swords. That's how the universe works – it's how the universe has *always* worked."

"But, Orion, you *are* the universe," you tell him. "Or part of it, at least. So why not make a change, break the mould, be the exception?"

The starry man frowns at your wise words.

"Well, I suppose I could give it a try," he replies. Orion looks at the terrified creature. "Hey, you, insignificant bear, please can I have my belt back?"

Timidly, the animal comes out from behind his marshmallow and takes off the belt.

"I didn't mean to upset you, Orion," he says, holding out the row of twinkling stars. "I thought we were playing a game. You can have your belt back, but first…I think the human needs *this*."

Taking the middle star from Orion's belt, the great bear places it into your hand. There's a picture of Miss Tentacle on one side and the number 178 on the other.

"A StoryQuest Star!" you cheer. "Wow, thank you. But I can't accept this – it belongs to Orion."

"Oh, don't worry about it," says the huntsman. He

fastens what's left of his belt around his waist. "As long as my trousers stop falling down, I'm happy. Just memorise the number then give the star to Miss Tentacle when you finish your quest to unlock the ultimate end to your story. Now get out of here, irrelevant mortal – a blackhole is no place for a human."

With that, Orion takes hold of the bus and hurls you out of the blackhole, where your spacecraft follows the path of a smouldering meteor through the starlit skies of the endless universe.

Congratulations, you've found the StoryQuest star!

Turn to page 154 to continue your quest.

"Excuse me," you call into the back of the bus, "do any of you live here, or have we landed on the wrong planet?"

One of the children stands up. She's green and hairy like a kiwi fruit, her mouth is bent up like a banana and her eyes are like two purple blackcurrants. What's more, you're fairly sure her legs are made out of rhubarb.

"Yes, we live here," she replies, nudging the identical aliens on either side of her. "But you have to buy us all donuts before we get off the bus – it's the law here. If we're caught outside without a donut, we'll be arrested by the Donut Police. Isn't that right, everyone?"

The other green aliens nod keenly.

BRIAN doesn't remember buying the aliens donuts before, but there are lots of things BRIAN doesn't remember. Do you want to buy them donuts, or tell them to get off the bus without any sugary treats?

I'd like to buy them all donuts. Turn to page 124.

Nope, they're not having any donuts. Turn to page 116.

You pull the rocket boost lever and your space-bus blasts forwards at the speed of light.

VROOSH!

You're pinned to the back of your seat as if stuck there with glue and BRIAN slides down the aisle like a bowling ball, hitting the back seat in a clatter of arms and legs.

"Are you hurt?" you call out, as the bus speeds on.

"That is like asking a dustbin lid if it has the toothache," replies the robot. "Please concentrate on steering the bus, young humanoid – the five moons will be difficult to navigate."

With a pull of the steering wheel, the nose of your spacecraft lifts and the bus hops over the first moon.

VROOSH!

You slam your foot on the accelerator and your spacecraft moves faster still. You miss the second moon by the skin of your tyres, as the next two swerve in at you from opposite directions.

VROOSH!

You steer left.

VROOSH!

You steer right.

VROOSH!

And your bus slides neatly between the two moons as your rocket boost comes to an end.

Suddenly, the fifth and final orb looms up from below the bus. It's huge, it's pink and it's right in your path, so you close your eyes and brace yourself for the impact, as the moon slams into your spacecraft.

GLOB-OB-OB-OB-OB!

But, wait a minute. That's not the sound of a moon crashing into a bus. That's the sound of a *trifle* crashing into a bus. And strangely, when you open your eyes, the world outside has turned pink and wobbly.

"W-where are we?" you stutter.

BRIAN picks herself up off the floor and moves to the front of the bus.

"The fifth moon appears to be made out of strawberry jelly," notes the robot. "It is not unusual for moons to be made out of edible substances, young humanoid. Cheese is the most common, but jelly is quite popular too. I believe the other moons of this planet are made out of bubble-gum."

Yum!

The weight of your bus is too heavy for the jelly-moon to hold up, so you're not stuck inside it for long. You slide through the gooey orb like a pebble through quicksand, moving down towards the bottom of the moon until finally slipping free with a very wobbly…

PWUCK-K-K-K-K!

Below, you see a holographic sign saying:

Miss Tentacle's School for Every Alien

A purple alien with pink candyfloss hair comes out of a metal building as you land on the dusty ground and climb out of the bus.

"Welcome to my school," smiles Miss Tentacle, "and congratulations on completing your quest – you are officially the best space navigator in the universe. Now, tell me, human, do you have the StoryQuest Star?"

If you have the StoryQuest Star, turn to the page number you saw twinkling on it when Orion handed it over.
If you don't have the star, don't worry – you're still an awesome StoryQuester! Turn to page 122.

Putting the space-bus in gear, you whizz after the flaming meteor. Smoke billows out from its hot surface, making your pathway difficult to navigate, but when the air clears a beautiful planet appears through the smog.

The planet looks a lot like Earth. It has green land, blue oceans and purple mountains, with wispy white clouds hanging over it like cobwebs. One side of the globe is lit by three sparkling suns, while the other lies in complete darkness.

Where would you like to land?

To land on the light side of the planet, turn to page 136.

To land on the dark side of the planet, turn to page 193.

The Triangular Sun sparkles in the near-distance like a glittering wedge of cheese. There's a silvery planet orbiting its highest point. It has fifteen yellow moons and a small space-rock hovering nearby.

On the rock, an old alien is sat on a deckchair. Her bottom is as wide as the rock and she looks like a giant potato, only more knobbly and without the mud. She's holding a big, red button and wearing a badge that reads:

Welcome to Sweatiolis.

You've found the second planet – cosmic!

"Who's that?" you whisper to BRIAN.

"She is a toll collector," the robot explains. "Sweatiolis has a silver forcefield to protect it from unwanted visitors. The toll collector will not open the barrier unless we pay her a fee."

As BRIAN searches her disc-drive for loose change, you pull up next to the rock and open the window.

The toll collector grimaces through the gap as she holds out her hand.

You don't have any money and it doesn't look like BRIAN does either.

How are you going to get past the grumpy toll collector?

I'll give her a sandwich from the lunchbox. Turn to page 131.

I'll talk nicely to her and explain what's happened. Turn to page 205.

The nebular is a long stretch of purple dust, hanging in space like a beautiful painting. You've never seen dust so lovely before.

At the centre of the nebular, there's a brilliant white light. You're not sure what it is – it could be an incredibly bright star, or it could be a luminous planet.

Do you want to take a closer look and find out?

Yes, please, let's fly closer and take a look. Turn to page 113.

Nah, that's okay, thanks – I'll follow the meteor instead. Turn to page 154.

The space station looks like an enormous spider hanging down from an invisible thread. There are no planets nearby, so you dock into the station to ask for directions.

An alien in a red uniform approaches your vehicle. He has a neck like a giraffe, curly hair and a face that looks as if somebody stood on it. He bends down to eye you through the open window of your bus.

"Hallo, hallo, hallo," he says, "what've we got 'ere then?"

This platform isn't just a space station. It's a space *police* station – the perfect place to ask for directions.

"Hello, officer," you smile. "I'm looking for a planet called Fruitopia. Would you mind telling me how to get there?"

"No problem," the officer replies. "But first things first. Driver's license, please," and he holds out a hand.

Uh oh. You didn't know you needed a license to fly a space-bus. What will you tell him?

I'll tell him the truth. Turn to page 105.
I'll make something up so I don't get into trouble.
Turn to page 189.

158

ZZZ-POP!

When you press the hologramophone button, Miss Tentacle appears in the aisle of the bus. She's covering up her tentacles with a towel and her candyfloss hair is as flat as a pancake. It looks like she just got out of the bath.

"Sorry to bother you," you say to the headmistress, "but I wanted to ask your advice. You see, I've dropped some of the children off at the Blue Moon Donut Café and—"

"*The Blue Moon Donut Café?!*" cries Miss Tentacle, almost dropping her towel. "There aren't any bus-stops by the Blue Moon Donut Café – you're on the wrong planet! You haven't given the Fruitopian children any donuts, have you?"

You watch as the children with the banana-mouths climb through the hatch of the café and start shovelling donuts into their faces.

"Erm, no, but—"

"Well, that's something at least," interrupts the headmistress. "Wait where you are and I'll send one of the teachers over to round up the children. Then it's back to Earth for you, human – we can't have you dropping children off on the wrong planets, there's too

159

much paperwork involved. Thanks for your help though. Now, where did I put my shampoo…"

The headmistress flickers out and your StoryQuest comes to an end. Try making a different choice and watch out for those pesky Fruitopian children – they're always up to no good!

Go back to the start of the book to try again, or turn to page 116 to make a different choice.

You take hold of the rocket boost lever and pull.

VROOSH!

Your bus shoots forwards at the speed of light, pinning you to the back of your seat, so you tilt the steering wheel and the nose of the spacecraft lifts. Your bus rushes to the surface of the water and bursts out through the rolling waves like a big, rectangular dolphin, where it shoots up past the island, away from the bus-stop, through the planet's atmosphere and into the darkness of space.

Wow, that rocket booster sure has got some welly!

A bit *too* much welly perhaps.

By the time the boost ends, you're fifty-two-billion lightyears away from the planet Aquavon. It's going to take six months for you to find your way back and the children's parents will all be quite cross when you get there. Have you considered emigrating to Venus? I hear it's nice there at this time of year.

Go back to the start of the book to try again, or turn to page 180 to make a different choice.

"Wakey wakey, rise and shine!" you call into the back of the bus. "You're home now! Up you get!"

The children of Noctron yawn loudly and stretch out their wings, so you open the doors and usher them through – perhaps being outside will wake them up a bit.

But as the sunlight hits their faces, the aliens curl up on the ground, fold their wings over their heads and go back to sleep. They're snoring happily and they won't wake up no matter how loudly you shout.

You're forced to tell Miss Tentacle, who immediately calls the Noctron-parents to collect their children. Oh, shucks!

Don't worry, StoryQuester – try this part of your challenge again and your mission will soon be complete.

Go back to the start of the book to try again, or turn to page 136 to make a different choice.

You're right – the shooty-beam-beams are harmless rays of light, and there's a small docking bay on the side of the spaceship, so you fly towards it and carefully land the bus.

You're greeted by a little green man with big ears. He leads you and BRIAN to the cockpit of the spaceship, where he addresses the rest of the crew.

"Arrived those from the bus they have," says the little green alien. "Cheeky nuisances with no respect for our shooty-beam-beams they are."

"Sorry, but we didn't mean to be cheeky," you reply. "We just stopped by to say hello. You see, I'm on a quest to return a group of alien school children back to their home planets and—"

"Well, *really!*" the golden android cuts in. At the sound of his voice, the yeti groans and puts his head in his paws. "Who in their right mind sends a young human being on a *quest*? It's ludicrous, that's what it is. Master Jake, are you hearing this?"

"Yes," sighs the man in the dressing gown, "I am *always* hearing you." He looks carefully at BRIAN. "Hey, you're a Bio-Robotic Intelligent Android Navigator, aren't you?"

"I am," the robot replies, "but you can call me

BRIAN. My memory box has been damaged in a meteor crash, so this young humanoid is helping me navigate the universe and return these children to their home planets."

The man thinks for a moment.

Then he turns to ask you a question.

"Say, kid, how'd you like to swap robots?"

Before you can answer, the golden android gasps dramatically.

"Swap me for a broken Bio-Robotic Intelligent Android Navigator?!" he cries. "Master Jake, you can't possibly mean that! Why would you want to *swap* me? All I ever do is look after you all! I cook, I clean, I mop the floor, I make the beds, I iron your dressing gowns, I polish the lasers, I put your glow-sticks on charge overnight, I make a lovely light chocolate soufflé with a raspberry jus…"

The woman flying the spaceship moves the currant buns over her ears as the android goes on with his list.

"Listen, kid," the man whispers, "*your* robot's damaged, but mine's as good as new. Look at him – he's all shiny and polished and not annoying at all. And his chocolate soufflé really *is* delicious."

"…I pull the yeti hairs from the plughole, I bake buns for the princess, I go, 'pyow-pyow-pyow,'

164

through the little microphone when we fire the shooty-beam-beams, I hide all the sharp kitchen utensils when your father visits…"

"See? You'd be crazy not to take me up on the offer," says the man. "Go on, kid – whadda you say?"

If you want to swap BRIAN for the android, turn to page 167.
If you want to keep BRIAN, turn to page 106.

When you ask BRIAN to steer your spacecraft through the five moons of Miss Tentacle's planet, the robot's eyes sparkle like jewels.

"I would *love* to drive the bus!" she beams. "Young humanoid, leave this to me."

Fasten your seat-belt, StoryQuester – you're about to find out why your satnav robot crashed this bus in the first place.

Taking the steering wheel, BRIAN places her *incredibly heavy iron foot* onto the accelerator (oh, dear) and…

THUD!

Her foot lands on the pedal like a tank falling off a cliff and the bus lurches forwards. It speeds into the path of the first moon, which pings your spacecraft across the galaxy and into the deepest, darkest realms of the outer cosmos.

You're lost in space and that's hard moon-cheese to swallow so close to the end of your quest, but don't give up now – Miss Tentacle is relying on you!

Go back to the start of the book to try again, or turn to page 120 to make a different choice.

"Okay," you reply, "I'll swap robots. But only if BRIAN's not upset about it."

"That is like asking a washing machine if it cries at sad films," remarks BRIAN, and she goes over to introduce herself to the yeti.

As you walk back to the docking bay, your shiny new android doesn't stop talking.

"Well, this is just lovely, isn't it?" he huffs. "You give people the best years of your life and what do they do? Swap you out like a library book, that's what. I've mopped these floors more times than I care to think of and I daren't even mention what I once had to clean from those toilets…"

The android goes on to tell you *exactly* what he cleaned from those toilets. He does tend to go on a bit, but at least he's not got a dent in his head.

When the android finally stops talking, you settle into the driver's seat and press the ignition button.

"Right then," you say, "which way to Sweatiolis?"

The android blinks with confusion.

"Why are you asking *me?* Doesn't this bus have a satnav robot?"

Your bus *did* have a satnav robot, but you just swapped her for a cleaning android. Which means

BRIAN is on the most epic space adventure the universe has ever known and you're stuck here with a talking vacuum cleaner.

You can't finish your quest without a satnav, StoryQuester, but Master Jake was right – the golden android really *does* make a yummy chocolate soufflé, so it's not all bad.

Nom, nom, nom!

Go back to the start of the book to try again, or turn to page 163 to make a different choice.

"Get back on the bus!" you call out to the young aliens. "We know you've been lying and we know we're on the wrong planet! If you don't come back, I'm calling Miss Tentacle to tell her what you've been up to!"

The mischievous aliens huff loudly. They crinkle their faces and narrow their little blackcurrant eyes. Then they stomp back onto the bus, sit down in their seats and fold their arms in a sulk.

The fruit-faced aliens are full of mischief and like playing tricks on people – you'd better keep an eye on them from now on.

Leaving the Blue Moon Donut Café, you decide to travel away from the giant star cluster to follow the golden comet instead. The icy orb leads you to a blue planet with a rippling surface. An immense ring circles around it, glittering in the light of a small, white sun.

It reminds you of Saturn.

But either you're seeing things or...*that ring has teeth!*

"Young humanoid," says BRIAN, "there is a giant space-eel guarding this planet. Space-eels are very rare and very dangerous. It will make entering the atmosphere quite tricky."

Okay, StoryQuester, how will you reach the planet without being eaten by the evil space-fish?

I'll fly quickly and take the space-eel by surprise. Turn to page 174.

I'll approach the eel slowly then swerve at the last second. Turn to page 197.

You pull the lunchbox out from under your seat and offer the toll collector a sandwich. The potatoey woman squints at it through narrowed eyes.

"Is that a sandwich?" she frowns.

"Of course it is not a sandwich," says BRIAN. "It is a cake."

That's strange. Why is your satnav robot lying about a sandwich?

"In that case," says the toll collector, "I suppose I could manage just one little bite. You'll still have to pay a fee though – nobody goes through the forcefield without paying a fee."

The alien's mouth starts to salivate. Then she helps herself to one of the sandwiches, takes a bite and...

POOF!

...vanishes in a flash of blinding light.

You stare in horror at the empty deckchair.

"What did we do to her?!" you cry. "Where did she go?! And why did you tell her that sandwich was a cake?!"

"If the toll collector had known it was a sandwich, young humanoid, she would not have eaten it," replies BRIAN. "Sandwiches have special teleportation powers in space – that tasty snack has transported the

171

toll collector to the other side of this galaxy, where she can no longer charge us a fee to land on this planet."

Awesome!

Something red catches your eye from the seat of the toll collector's deckchair – it's the forcefield button! You reach out, take hold of the object and press. The silvery exterior of the planet opens up like an elevator door as the forcefield unlocks.

Double awesome!

But as Sweatiolis emerges from beneath it like a big, rusty ball-bearing, the heat of the Triangular Sun becomes almost unbearable. You'll have to cool down the air inside the bus if you want to land, otherwise you'll be roasted to a crisp.

Triple awe—

No, wait. That's not awesome at all.

What are you going to do?

To turn on the air-conditioning, turn to page 191.

To open the windows and create a breeze, turn to page 203.

"Thanks, but we don't have time for donuts," you say to the human-like alien. "I'm on a quest to take these children back to their home planets, but I can't find the bus-stop. Do you know where it is?"

"There ain't no bus-stops on the Planet of the Blue Moon," sings the man. "There ain't no bus-stops by order of the King, uh huh huh."

His left leg wiggles with a life of its own and his top lip curls up like an old sandwich. This guy is pottier than a plant pot. You're not sure he knows where his elbow is, let alone where the bus-stop is.

Will you believe the crazy donut seller and leave this planet, or ask the school children if you're in the right place?

I'll trust the donut seller, leave this planet and follow the golden comet instead. Turn to page 119.

I'd like to ask the school children if we're in the right place. Turn to page 150.

You point the bus at the eel's face and slam your foot on the accelerator.

VROOSH!

Hearing the roar of your engine, the creature turns with surprise. Giant eels are used to spaceships flying *away* from them, not *towards* them, and the bonnet of your bus is heading right for the middle of its face.

The creature's eyes bulge like gobstoppers, until suddenly, at the very last second, it ducks out of the way and you slide down its slippery back like a penny on ice.

WHEEEEEEE!

Down and down you spiral, away from the eel's head and off the end of its tail, into the atmosphere of the glistening blue planet.

Whoa, excellent driving skills, StoryQuester!

As you swoop through the cloudy sky, you realise this planet is a giant ball of crystal-clear water. The only land is a small island with the hologram of a bus hovering over it. It's a bus-stop, and it looks like you've found your first planet.

Cosmic!

But landing a bus on that tiny little island is going

to be tricky.

Do you want to try?

Yes, please – let's do this! Turn to page 180.

No, thanks – let's not! Turn to page 190.

You've never inspected a bus before, but there doesn't seem to be anything wrong with it. At the back of the bus, there are no dents, no bits hanging off it, not even so much as a scratch, and you're about to give up when something yellow catches your eye.

Cripes! There's a bunch of bananas stuck in the exhaust pipe – so *that's* why it wouldn't start. Those pesky Fruitopian children must have put them there.

When you've unblocked the exhaust pipe and eaten a yummy banana or two, you're back in the velvety skies of the infinite universe and on your way to the final planet.

BRIAN presses the satnav button on her arm.

"The next bus-stop we must find is on a planet called Noctron," she says. "To locate the planet Noctron, we must bear left – *BLEEP!* Bear left – *BLEEP!* Bear left – *BLEEP!* Bear left – *BLEEP!*"

That's strange. This is the first time BRIAN has only given you *one* direction. And if you turn left, you'll be gobbled up by the same blackhole you were so careful to avoid earlier on.

"I'm not sure bearing left is a good idea, BRIAN," you reply. "Perhaps we could go right instead, or—"

"No!" cries the robot, her antenna buzzing. "Bear

left! Bear left! Bear left! Young humanoid, *there is a bear on our left!"*

Through the window, you see a giant bear made of stars running through space. The creature is going into the blackhole and he's beckoning you with his big sparkly paw.

Do you want to follow him?

A space-bear? Cool! Let's follow him! Turn to page 146.

A space-bear? Eek! Let's get out of here! Turn to page 125.

"You've found the StoryQuest Star!" smiles Miss Tentacle. "That's wonderful news. Now, I believe we have one last home planet to visit – come along, human, I'll fly you back to Earth in my private space-jet."

The headmistress leads you to a shiny spacecraft. It has twelve rocket boosters, a golden rudder and a little red flag on its nose. It looks like you'll be travelling home in style.

Miss Tentacle climbs into the jet as you take the seat next to her.

"Thanks for the brilliant adventure, BRIAN," you call from the window, with a wave of your hand. "I hope we meet again someday."

"I'm sure we will meet again soon," smiles the robot. "But for now, goodbye, young humanoid."

You take to the starlit skies for one last time, soaring back through the infinite universe, until planet Earth appears in the distance. Miss Tentacle lands at your usual bus-stop. Your mum's still standing there, her mouth's still hanging open and her face is still grey (and it goes a bit greyer when the betentacled headmistress follows you out of the space-jet).

Miss Tentacle tosses the StoryQuest Star into the

air like a coin, where it hangs over your head, spinning in circles, until suddenly, with a bright flash of light, it turns into the flickering hologram of a bus.

"I don't understand," you say. "Why is there an intergalactic bus-stop here on Earth?"

"It's for you," smiles the alien. "Let's call it a little thank you gift. BRIAN's memory will be fixed by tomorrow morning and *this* will be one of her stops. I'd like *you* to be the first human child to attend Miss Tentacle's School for Every Alien."

Your spine tingles with excitement.

"Cosmic!" you cry, gazing up at the glittering hologram, and as your mum's face turns greyer than a cloudy day on the dark side of Noctron, you realise waiting at a bus-stop isn't quite so boring after all.

Congratulations! You've found the ultimate end to your story and tomorrow morning you'll be the first human to attend Miss Tentacle's School for Every Alien. Wowsers! You're a StoryQuest hero!

If you'd like to read more StoryQuest adventure books, take a look in the back of this book.

As your bus swoops down towards the tiny island, you realise the target is even smaller than it first appeared. Landing a bus on it will be like trying to fit an elephant on a postage stamp.

And so, clinging tightly to the steering wheel you plummet towards the planet, where you miss the island and nosedive into the water.

SPLASH!

Your bus sinks like a boulder. The windows are closed and there's plenty of air, but the frame of your spacecraft creaks under the weight of the water as you drop towards the seabed.

An eerie light shines up through the murky shadows. There's something down there, something huge, and as the haze clears an underwater city emerges. Its buildings are lit by lilac-coloured streetlamps and pebbled roads wind in and out of the algae-covered parks.

You land in the middle of a town square. The aliens who live here stop what they're doing to gawp up at this unexpected arrival. They have silvery skin, flippers for feet and their eyes are the size of footballs.

Five children waddle to the front of the bus. They tap on the door with their flippers.

"I'm sorry," you tell them, "but I can't open the door underwater. I won't be able to breathe. We need to get back to the surface so I can let you out."

To activate the automatic tyre inflator, turn to page 111.

If you'd rather use your rocket-booster, turn to page 161.

A giant space-eel is scarier than a maths teacher with an algebra test, but bravely you face the beast and slowly press the accelerator.

The eel sees you. Its eyes narrow. It licks its gelatinous lips as a wicked smile creeps over its face. A bus full of children is like a tasty tin of baked beans to a giant space-eel and he wants you all in his belly.

Nom, nom, nom!

The monster opens its huge jaws and a bus-rattling roar blasts out of its mouth.

GRAAAAAAW!

As its teeth snap closed, you swerve left, whizz past its head and enter the planet's atmosphere. You should be safe in here – the eel can't leave the realms of its outer-space home.

But suddenly, the terrible beast whips out a tongue the size of Italy and wraps it around your bus like a frog catching a fly. A gloop of space-eel spit seeps in through an open window as you're pulled away from the planet and into the eel's mouth. It drips onto your lap like an unset jelly and then...

GULP!

The world goes dark.

Luckily, your bus is too crunchy for the space-eel to chew, so it swallows you whole and no-one gets hurt. You'll pass through the creature's digestive system in two to three days, along with everything else it has eaten today, by which time the children's parents will be sick with worry.

Try taking the huge fish by surprise on your next attempt, StoryQuester, and you'll soon be on your way to Aquatron.

Go back to the start of the book to try again, or turn to page 184 to make a different choice.

"Donuts all round, please," you say to the human-like man in the diner. "But after that we really must get on with finding our first bus-stop."

"No problem, kid." He hands you a box of the sugary treats, then picks up a smaller container. "And this one's just for you."

Inside the container you find a double-layered, chocolate covered donut with rainbow sprinkles.

"For me?" you gasp. "But why?"

"There ain't no bus-stops on the Planet of the Blue Moon, kid," he whispers, "so I reckon you're on the wrong planet. But this donut sandwich should put you back in the right place. Just eat it, then follow the golden comet."

This guy is crazy. You have no idea what he's talking about, but you take the donut sandwich and thank him for the advice. As the whiff of chocolatey gooiness drifts up your nose, you lift the sandwich up to your mouth, sink your teeth in and…

POOF!

The world around you vanishes in a blinding flash of light and you find yourself back in the velvety skies of outer-space.

"W-what happened?" you gasp. "Where's the

diner gone?"

"The diner has not gone anywhere," replies BRIAN. "That donut sandwich has teleported our spacecraft to the other side of the galaxy. We seem to be back where we started, young humanoid."

Whoa, that was the best donut sandwich *ever!*

A golden comet glitters across the sky. You remember the words of the man in the diner and smile, steering your space-bus towards it.

The comet leads you to a blue planet with a rippling surface. A huge ring circles around it, sparkling in the light of a small, white sun. It reminds you of Saturn, but either you're seeing things or...*that ring has teeth!*

"Young humanoid," says BRIAN, "there is a giant space-eel guarding this planet. Space-eels are very rare and very dangerous. It will make entering the atmosphere quite tricky."

Okay, StoryQuester, how will you reach the planet without being eaten by the evil space-fish?

I'll fly quickly and take the space-eel by surprise. Turn to page 174.

I'll approach the eel slowly then swerve at the last second. Turn to page 182.

You press the orange button and…

SQUEEEEAK!

…the big windscreen wiper on the front of your bus drags painfully over the glass.

Marvellous!

"You have excellent button-choosing skills," remarks the police officer, "the best I've ever seen, in fact. I can't tell you how many people press the ejector seat button instead of the wipers. Anyway, here's your license."

He hands you a certificate with gold writing on it.

"Thank you," you say. "Can you tell us how to get to Fruitopia now please?"

"I sure can," replies the police officer, pointing towards the blackhole. "Just fly past that deadly tunnel of darkness and Fruitopia will be on your left," and with that, the officer goes back to his work.

Leaving the police station, you notice a stream of stars disappearing into the churning depths of the blackhole. It pulls at your bus as you fly towards it, but you keep your distance and somehow manage to pass by unharmed.

Phew!

Beyond the blackhole, there's an orange. That's

right – an orange. An *actual* orange, only the size of a planet. There's even an apple-moon orbiting its stem.

With no toll collectors or space-eels blocking your path, you enter the planet's atmosphere and find yourself in a world made entirely of fruit.

It's quite a sight and it smells delicious. The trees have bananas for trunks, the houses are made out of coconuts, the mountains are kiwis and the pavements are lined with slices of pear. And there, next to the cherry-juice river, is a holographic bus-stop.

You've found the planet Fruitopia – cosmic!

With a squelch, you land on the sticky ground. The five alien children with furry green skin bounce to the front of the bus. They jump through the open doorway, run past their parents then disappear around the back of the bus.

"Wow, that was easy," you smile. "Okay, BRIAN, only one planet left – onto the next bus-stop!"

You press the ignition button to fire-up the engine.

CHUG...

CHUG...

CHUG...

CHUG...

But the bus won't start.

"The children of Fruitopia are well-known for making mischief," notes BRIAN. "I fear they have played a trick on us by somehow disabling our spacecraft."

Oo, the little scallywags!

What will you do, StoryQuester?

I'll get out and see if I can fix it. Turn to page 176.
Hm, let's pull the rocket booster lever – that should do it. Turn to page 135.

You decide to make something up so you don't get into trouble.

"I can't show you my license," you say to the officer. "Because, erm, my robot ate it."

BRIAN scratches her dented head.

"Did I?" she frowns. "I do not remember that. I am terribly sorry, young humanoid. What an awful thing for me to do."

The police officer wrinkles his face to the size of a prune. Then he puts a pair of handcuffs on BRIAN's wrists.

"Eating somebody's driver's license is a very serious offence," he tells the robot. "You'll have to come into the station for questioning, I'm afraid."

Oh, no! You told a lie and now BRIAN is being taken into custody for eating your imaginary driver's license. Quick, StoryQuester, go back and make a different choice before your robot ends up behind bars!

Go back to the start of the book to try again, or turn to page 158 to make a different choice.

Instead of landing on the tiny island, you hover your bus close to the land and open the doors. The five scaly aliens who live on Aquavon waddle along the aisle, waving their flippers and chattering like dolphins, as one by one they leap out of the bus and into the water.

A shoal of parents bobs up through the waves. They smile, waving their fins in thanks, before taking their amphibious children down to their underwater home. You've taken the first group of children back to their home planet – great work, StoryQuester!

BRIAN congratulates you with a bleep of joy, then she presses the satnav button at the top of her arm.

"The second bus-stop we must find is on a planet called Sweatiolis," she says. "To locate the planet Sweatiolis we must travel towards the Triangular Sun – *BLEEP!* We should chase the shooting star - *BLEEP!* Travel towards the Triangular Sun - *BLEEP!* Chase the shooting star – *BLEEP!*" Where to next, mighty StoryQuester?

To go towards the Triangular Sun, turn to page 155.

To chase the shooting star, turn to page 140.

You decide to turn on the air-conditioning, so you flick the switch and an icy breeze fills the bus.

Ah, that's better!

But the hairy children who live here run to the front of the spacecraft. Their teeth are chattering and they're shivering like bald camels on an ice-berg. They're used to the soaring temperatures of Sweatiolis and the air-conditioning is making them chilly.

"I can see the bus-stop below us," you tell them. "I'll land quickly before you get too cold," and soon your bus touches down on the dusty ground.

With a hiss, the doors open. The children dash out into the raging heat, where their long hair suddenly drops out to reveal five scorpion-like aliens.

Wowee! You've returned the second group of children to their home planet and are officially marvellous!

BRIAN presses the satnav button on her arm and your quest goes on.

"The third bus-stop we must find is on a planet called Fruitopia," she says. "To locate the planet Fruitopia, we must travel towards the blackhole – *BLEEP!* We should head towards the space station – *BLEEP!* Travel towards the blackhole – *BLEEP!* Head towards the space station -*BLEEP!*"

Which one of BRIAN's instructions will you follow *this* time, StoryQuester?

Let's head towards the space station. Turn to page 158.

Let's travel towards the blackhole. Turn to page 144.

Your bus plunges into the thick darkness like a cherry into a trifle. Wow, it's creepy here! But the last group of children stirs in their sleep as you land with a bump on the grassy planet.

Yawning, they move down the aisle and towards the open doorway. A hologram of a bus flickers alight and a group of bat-like parents waves as their nocturnal children fly eagerly off the bus.

Do you know what this means, StoryQuester? It means you've taken *all* of the children safely back to their home planets and are officially the most spectacular space navigator in the history of the cosmos.

All you have to do now is take the bus back to—

BEEP! BEEP! BEEP! BEEP! BEEP!

Take the bus back to school and your quest will be—

BEEP! BEEP! BEEP! BEEP! BEEP!

And your quest will be—

BEEP! BEEP! BEEP! BEEP! BEEP!

Your quest will—

BEEP! BEEP! BEEP! BEEP! BEEP!

What in Jupiter's name is that awful beeping noise?

A red light illuminates on the dashboard. Your

fuel tank is almost empty and you might not have enough power to fly back to Miss Tentacle's School for Every Alien without filling-up.

"There is a space fuel station not far from here," notes BRIAN, with a press of her satnav button. "But it sells a different type of fuel to the one I use in this bus. There is a chance it will work well. But there is also a chance the new fuel will cause our bus to evaporate into a gazzilion tiny droplets of molten metal."

Blimey.

Well, this is quite a pickle. Will you risk filling-up with the new fuel, or see if you can make it back to school without it?

I'll carry on without filling up. Turn to page 134.
I'd like to go to the fuel station please. Turn to page 120.

As you steer your bus towards the giant star-cluster, a rocky planet appears in the distance. It's orbiting a tiny sun and a pale blue moon hangs in the hazy sky.

You drive closer. Could this be the planet you're looking for? There's definitely life here, although most of the buildings look really old-fashioned. There are neon signs in the windows and the sound of rock 'n' roll music is blasting out of their doors.

You see a row of spaceships next to a sign saying THE BLUE MOON DONUT CAFE and realise you've landed in the drive-through of an intergalactic diner.

Awesome!

There's a serving hatch to your right, so you open a window and lean out. A human-like alien with slicked-back hair and an upturned collar picks up a microphone, clears his throat and sings, "Welcome to the Blue Moon Donut Café. What can I get cha, uh huh huh?"

BRIAN's head appears over your left shoulder.

"Young humanoid," she says, "I do not think we should stop for donuts – we have not even located our first bus-stop yet."

She's right.

You know she's right.

But…*space-donuts?* They sound delicious!

Do you want to order some?

Yes, please – there's always time for donuts! Turn to page 184.

No, thank you – I'll ask the alien if we're on the right planet and get on with my quest. Turn to page 173.

A giant space-eel is scarier than a maths teacher with an algebra test, but bravely you face the beast and slowly press the accelerator.

The eel sees you. Its eyes narrow. It licks its gelatinous lips as a wicked smile creeps over its face. A bus full of children is like a tasty tin of baked beans to a giant space-eel and he wants you all in his belly.

Nom, nom, nom!

The monster opens its huge jaws and a bus-rattling roar blasts out of its mouth.

GRAAAAAAW!

As its teeth snap closed, you swerve left, whizz past its head and enter the planet's atmosphere. You should be safe in here – the eel can't leave the realms of its outer-space home.

But suddenly, the terrible beast whips out a tongue the size of Italy and wraps it around your bus like a frog catching a fly. A gloop of space-eel spit seeps in through an open window as you're pulled away from the planet and into the eel's mouth. It drips onto your lap like an unset jelly and then…

GULP!

The world goes dark.

Luckily, your bus is too crunchy for the space-eel to chew, so it swallows you whole and no-one gets hurt. You'll pass through the creature's digestive system in two to three days, along with everything else it has eaten today, by which time the children's parents will be sick with worry.

Try taking the huge fish by surprise on your next attempt, StoryQuester, and you'll soon be on your way to Aquatron.

Go back to the start of the book to try again, or turn to page 169 to make a different choice.

A giant space-eel is scarier than a maths teacher with an algebra test, but bravely you turn to the beast and slowly press the accelerator.

The eel sees you. Its eyes narrow. It licks its gelatinous lips as a wicked smile creeps over its face. A bus full of children is like a tasty tin of baked beans to a giant space-eel and he wants you all in his belly.

Nom, nom, nom!

The monster opens its huge jaws and a bus-rattling roar blasts out of its mouth.

GRAAAAAAW!

As its teeth snap closed, you swerve left, whizz past its head and enter the planet's atmosphere. You should be safe here – the eel can't leave the realms of its outer-space home.

But suddenly, the terrible beast whips out a tongue the size of Italy and wraps it around your bus like a frog catching a fly. A gloop of space-eel spit seeps in through an open window as you're pulled away from the planet and into the eel's mouth. It drips onto your lap like an unset jelly and then…

GULP!

The world goes dark.

Luckily, your bus is too crunchy for the space-eel to chew, so it swallows you whole and no-one gets hurt. You'll pass through the creature's digestive system in two to three days, along with everything else it has eaten today, by which time the children's parents will be sick with worry.

Try taking the huge fish by surprise on your next attempt, StoryQuester, and you'll soon be on your way to Aquatron.

Go back to the start of the book to try again, or turn to page 119 to make a different choice.

You decide to talk nicely to the toll collector and explain what happened.

"Hello," you say. "Erm, how are you?"

The alien smiles.

Actually, it could be a snarl.

Whatever it is, it looks like it hurts.

"Nrgh," growls the toll collector.

"I, erm, really like your clothes," you go on. "They're very—"

But then you realise she's a talking potato and she's not wearing any clothes. Awkward.

The toll collector pushes her hand closer towards you.

"You gotta pay," she says, "so gimme your money or *CLEAR OFF!*"

The force of her voice ruffles your hair and a drop of alien spit lands on your face.

"The thing is," you say, wiping it off with the back of your hand, "I'm on a quest to save these children, but I don't have any money. Please can you press the button and let me through without paying? Just this once?"

The toll collector curls her rubbery lips up under her nose and looks carefully into your eyes. Then she

shoves the forcefield button into her mouth and crunches it up like a boiled sweet.

CHOMP! CHOMP! CHOMP!

You take that as a 'no.'

The forcefield won't be opening any time soon, not now the button is inside the toll collector's belly, so you can't get to Sweatiolis to return the second group of children. Never mind, StoryQuester – why not go back and see if the toll collector would like a nice sandwich instead?

Go back to the start of the book to try again, or turn to page 129 to make a different choice.

When you open the window, a terrible stink fills the bus. It smells worse than a cabbage-eating skunk in a sewer.

"Phooey!" you cry, pinching your nose. "What's that horrible smell?"

"I believe the pong you're referring to comes from the fifteen moons of Sweatiolis," says BRIAN. "They are made out of cheese and are well-known for their astronomical whiff."

The stinky air makes your head dizzy and your vision blurred. You can't see to drive, so BRIAN presses the hologramophone button and the headmistress appears in the aisle of the bus, snoring like an elephant with a trumpet stuck up its nostril.

"ZZZZZZ! ZZZZZZ! ZZZZ- Oh, erm, hello," she splutters. "I was just resting my eyes." She wasn't. She was snoring like an elephant. "How can I help you?"

"Miss Tentacle, I am afraid the young humanoid has opened a window near the fifteen moons of Sweatiolis," explains BRIAN, "and the terrible whiff of cheese is overpowering their senses."

"That's awful news," says Miss Tentacle. "We must take the human back to an Earthean doctor as soon as possible. Wait there, BRIAN – I'll send someone out to fetch you."

A tow-ship arrives. It pulls you back to your home planet, where the doctor says you'll be fine but the smell lingers on you for weeks and everyone at school thinks you stepped in something a dog did.

Go back to the start of the book to try again, or turn to page 171 to make a different choice.

You decide to talk nicely to the toll collector and explain what happened.

"Hello," you say. "Erm, how are you?"

The alien smiles.

Actually, it could be a snarl.

Whatever it is, it looks like it hurts.

"Nrgh," growls the toll collector.

"I, erm, really like your clothes," you go on. "They're very—"

But then you realise she's a talking potato and she's not wearing any clothes. Awkward.

The toll collector pushes her hand closer towards you.

"You gotta pay," she says, "so gimme your money or *CLEAR OFF!*"

The force of her voice ruffles your hair and a drop of alien spit lands on your face.

"The thing is," you say, wiping it off with the back of your hand, "I'm on a quest to save these children, but I don't have any money. Please can you press the button and let me through without paying? Just this once?"

The toll collector curls her rubbery lips up under her nose and looks carefully into your eyes. Then she

shoves the forcefield button into her mouth and crunches it up like a boiled sweet.

CHOMP! CHOMP! CHOMP!

You take that as a 'no.'

The forcefield won't be opening any time soon, not now the button is inside the toll collector's belly, so you can't get to Sweatiolis to return the second group of children. Never mind, StoryQuester – why not go back and see if the toll collector would like a sandwich instead?

Go back to the start of the book to try again, or turn to page 155 to make a different choice.

THE GOOD, THE BAD AND THE

SHERIFF'S

HORSE

Choose the page - Unlock the adventure

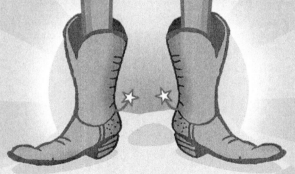

A StoryQuest book by

BECCI MURRAY

STORYQUEST

CHOOSE THE PAGE - UNLOCK THE ADVENTURE

ISBN: 978-1-9162069-4-6

Published by Llama House Children's Books

Welcome to your StoryQuest challenge, the book where YOU are in charge of what happens and YOU are the star of the adventure.

Start your quest on the first page, where your challenge will be explained. At the end of each chapter you'll find two options – choose a page to decide what you want to do next.

As a bonus feature, every StoryQuest book has a SPECIAL CHARACTER hidden amongst the pages. Find the character, and they'll give you a STORYQUEST STAR. This will help you unlock the ultimate ending to your adventure.

There are SO many different paths and SO many different endings – some are good, some are bad, some are happy, some are sad. Which will you choose? Will you complete the challenge? And where will your story end?

Good luck, intrepid StoryQuester, and happy reading!

Shovelling horse poo for pocket money sure does stink. It's worse than wiping tables at the ol' saloon. It's worse than bending horseshoes for the local blacksmith. It's even worse than untangling rope at Lassos 'R' Us.

But this is the Wild West, this is the Sheriff's horse poo and being a stablehand sure beats working for a rustler or a bandit. Here comes the Sheriff now on his horse. He's practising his riding skills for this evening's rodeo.

"Howdy, Sheriff!" you call from the stable.

"Howdy, partner!" smiles the Sheriff, with a wave of his hat. "Mighty fine day for a rodeo, and ain't that the truth. Yee-haw!"

Lightning Bolt is a very skilled horse. Cowgirls and boys come from all over the Wild West to watch him compete in the barrel-race at the annual Maintown Rodeo. And he always, *always* wins.

But this morning, as Lightning Bolt enters the paddock, you notice he's walking a little strangely. He's wriggling like a prairie-dog with fleas, he's squirming like a snake on the hot desert sand, he's kicking his legs like a bucking bronco, and although the Sheriff tries to hold on, he's thrown from his saddle with a loud, "Yee-haaAAAAAARGH!" where he lands in the big pile of poo you just shovelled out of the stable.

SPLAT!

"Sheriff!" you cry, running to pull him out. "What's wrong with your horse?"

The man sighs as he wipes the poo from his eye.

"We giddy-upped into a cactus out west," he replies. "Lightnin' Bolt prickled his bee-hind and caught the Itchity Fever. He'll be all tickly-scratchy for weeks."

"But it's the rodeo tonight," you remind him. "Everyone will be so disappointed if you don't compete. What are you going to do?"

"Ain't much I *can* do," sighs the Sheriff. "Course, my Great Grandpappy Pete woulda cured him in no time. He was a medicine man and he had a recipe for an Itchity Fever medicine. But I can't go skedaddlin' all over the Wild West lookin' for ingredients – not when there's a rodeo to set up." The Sheriff pauses. His eyes sparkle and the corners of his moustache twitch. "I don't suppose *you* could look for 'em instead?"

"*Me?!*" you gasp. "But, Sheriff, travelling out of town isn't safe. The Wild West is ruled by thieves and bandits, not to mention all those snakes and jackals and goats I'd run into." (Yes, even the *goats* of the Wild

212

West are dangerous.) You sigh heavily. "Although, I suppose anything's better than shovelling poo. I'll do it!"

"Yee-haw!" cheers the Sheriff. "Thanks, kid! There are three ingredients you'll need to find: a pint of buffalo milk, a fresh dragon fruit, and the feather of a Four-Legged Duck."

(Sorry, did he just say, *the feather of a Four-Legged Duck?*)

The Sheriff whistles and a scruffy mule ambles in from a neighbouring field.

"You can borrow my ol' pal Tumbleweed to speed up your journey. There's hay in her saddlebag but eatin' it makes her windier than a desert typhoon – you'll do well to remember that. And don't go losin' her, or you won't make it back in time for the rodeo."

"Don't lose the mule," you repeat. "Got it."

The Sheriff takes a book out of his pocket.

"This notebook belonged to my Great Grandpappy Pete. He drew pictures of the all ingredients he used in his medicines and a map of the Wild West to help him find 'em. You can take it with you. And here are some coins and my divination stick too." You put the items into your saddlebag and the Sheriff raises a bushy eyebrow. "So, are you ready for your StoryQuest to begin?"

A surge of determination shoots from the soles of your boots to the top of your hat.

"Yee-haw!" you cry. "I'm ready, Sheriff!"

"Then saddle-up, partner, and remember – *do not lose the mule* or you won't make it back in time for the rodeo," and with that, you head out onto the perilous plains of the Wild West on a quest to save the Sheriff's horse.

Your StoryQuest has begun! Turn to page 259.

You take the divination stick out of your saddlebag in the hope of finding water. It looks like a large twig with a forked end. You've no idea how it works, so you hold it up in the air and watch it carefully, as Tumbleweed trots to the northernmost side of the desert.

"This is ridiculous," you mutter, more than an hour later. "How on earth can a *stick* tell us where to find water? I mean, I've heard some tall stories in my time, but I've never heard anything sillier than a twig that can find—"

SPLASH!

You were so busy looking up at the divination stick, you didn't notice Blue River right there in front of you. It's definitely *wet* enough here for ducks, but there are none in sight. So you wade across to the other side and climb onto the bank, where Tumbleweed shakes herself like a wet dog.

In front of you lies a dense forest known as Green Woodland. It's as good a place as any to search for a Four-Legged Duck, so you venture into the trees.

Before long, you come across a make-shift tent; a big sheet of canvas thrown over a low branch. A scruffy-looking man crawls out. He has a full beard, shoulder-length hair and eyebrows you could tie knots in.

At first you think he's a yeti, but then you decide he must be a hermit. Do you want to talk to him about Four-Legged Ducks?

Yes, please – he looks like an intelligent sort of chap. Turn to page 281.

No, thank you – he looks proper scary. Turn to page 308.

You lean right and the raft drifts east, where the river carries you through the great fir trees of Green Woodland. You can hear the birds singing and feel the gentle rocking of the water, and you think to yourself, "Ah yes, StoryQuesting is the life for me."

But there's a bend in the river. And suddenly you're thrown into a long stretch of white-water rapids, where you're tossed around by the raging current like a stone in a cowboy's boot.

You cling to the raft with both hands, but Tumbleweed can't keep her footing. Your mule's about to fall into the water – you'll need to do something and fast!

To shout for help, turn to page 256.
To throw Tumbleweed to safety, turn to page 267.

The summit of Purple Mountain is too steep for a mule, so you tie Tumbleweed to a tree as you start the difficult climb.

Wow, the air's thin up here! But you move fast and eventually reach the summit. From here, you have a breath-taking view of the Wild West. You can see Crabbity Jack's Shack below you and Blue River running alongside it, then beyond that the arid Wilderness with Maintown at its centre.

Now you know *exactly* how to get home!

Yee-haw!

Hurriedly, you scramble down the rocky slope and run to the tree where you left your mule. But Tumbleweed isn't there! Someone must have untied her! And as you scan the side of the mountain, a terrible sound fills the air.

MEHHHHHHHHHHHHH!

You turn suddenly and find yourself face to face with the scariest, rottenest, grisliest band of villains in the whole of the Wild West. *Goats!* A huge heard of them! They've chewed through Tumbleweed's reins and they're holding her captive in the trunk of a hollowed-out sycamore tree.

You're terrified (and who wouldn't be?), but

you've come too far to give up and no wonky-toothed farmyard bandits are going to stand between you and that mule.

Bravely, you march towards the tree stump with your head held high. The goats circle around you, scuffing the ground and chewing the air with menace. When you duck inside the hollowed trunk, they think you're surrendering to their supreme goatiness. But then you snatch a handful of hay out of Tumbleweed's saddlebag and the herd panics.

Their eyes bulge like gobstoppers and the biggest goat makes a dash for the tree, so you quickly feed Tumbleweed the hay, take hold of her saddle and…

PAAAARRRRRRRRRRRRRP!

The mule's windy bottom sends the pair of you shooting out of the trunk like a big, furry cannonball, scattering goats in every direction as you whiz down the side of Purple Mountain, across Blue River, through the Wilderness and into the centre of Maintown, where you land in a crumpled heap in the Sheriff's stable.

Wow, that was some mule-ride, partner!

With no time to lose before the rodeo starts, you grab the mucking-out bucket and pour in the buffalo milk. Then you squeeze in the juice from the fresh dragon fruit and drop the beautifully striped feather into the mix.

At once, something wonderful happens. Little multicoloured bubbles rise to the surface of the mixture. They float up out of the bucket and then burst into tiny rainbows, each one falling back into the medicine like blossom as the feather crumbles into a sparkling, golden dust.

Your Itchity Fever medicine is ready! Yee-haw!

Hurriedly, you run outside to the paddock with your bucket. Lightning Bolt is itching himself on a tree, but with a little encouragement you persuade him to taste the mixture. He likes it. In fact, he likes it *so* much that he drinks the whole bucketful and burps out the biggest rainbow you've ever seen.

BAAAAAAAAAAAAAARP!

A beautiful arc of colours stretches out across the Wild West and the Sheriff's horse stops wriggling.

You've cured Lightning Bolt of his Itchity Fever and are the most magnificent StoryQuester that ever lived! But will you tell the Sheriff your good news *before the rodeo*, or surprise him at the barrel-race?

To tell the Sheriff before the rodeo, turn to page 292.

To take Lightning-Bolt straight to the rodeo as a surprise, turn to page 246.

Great Grandpappy Pete's Drawings of Medicinal Feathers

The feather of a Long-Nosed Peacock is good for patients who are being sat on by a horse. A doctor should use the feather to tickle the animal under its armpit or on the foot. This will make the horse giggle so much it will fall off the patient. Please note, finding the armpit of an animal without arms can often prove tricky.

The feather of a Sabre-Toothed Robin is an excellent treatment for patients who are stuck in the swing-door of a saloon. The medically trained person should drop the feather near the patient, shouting, "Argh! A Sabre-Toothed Robin! We're all goners!" and the patient will immediately unstick themselves from the door and run off down the street.

The feather of a Four-Legged Duck is known for its use on patients who prickle themselves on a cactus. It can be mixed with a pint of buffalo milk and the juice of a fresh dragon fruit and used as an effective cure for Itchity Fever.

You've learnt what the feather of a Four-Legged Duck looks like! Turn to page 251 to continue your quest.

You go to the local store to buy a new bowl. The bell goes *TING!* as you open the door and a middle-aged woman stands up behind the counter.

"Howdy," she smiles. Her messy hair and prickly chin remind you of a cactus. "I'm Mrs Bullwinkle. Welcome to Maintown Store. What can I get you?"

"I'd like to buy a mixing bowl, please," you reply.

Mrs Bullwinkle lifts a ceramic pot down from one of the shelves and places it onto the counter.

"You're lucky," she says, as you pick up the bowl. "It's my last one. That'll be two gold coins, please."

But you don't have any coins. You used them all getting into the rodeo.

"Erm, would you mind if I paid you later, please?" you ask sheepishly, your face going a little red.

"Yes, I do mind!" snaps the storekeeper. "If you ain't got no money, you can get outta my store. Go on, clear off!"

Mrs Bullwinkle makes a grab for the bowl.

Instinctively, you pull it away.

And…

CRASH!

It slips out of your hands and smashes all over the floor.

Mrs Bullwinkle is furious. Her prickly chin turns red and bristly, as she runs out from behind the counter and locks the door. She won't let you out of her store until you've pieced the whole thing back together again, by which time the rodeo will have finished.

Well, ain't that a pain in the neckerchief?

Bad luck, partner.

Go back to the start of the book to try again, or turn to page 276 to make a different choice.

You trot down the crumbling slopes of Dead Man's Gorge, fanning yourself with your hat. It's even hotter here than it was in the Wilderness. This side of Grey Rock catches the most sunlight at this time of day and the heat is unbearable.

The mule's feet are already starting to drag.

She might get sunstroke if you don't take shelter.

To the east of Dead Man's Gorge is a disused gold mine. It's a large stone building with broken windows and no door. You could go inside to get out of the sun, but it's kind of spooky-looking and you can already see Ancient Annie's Buffalo Farm in the distance.

Will you carry on, or take shelter in the old mine?

To shelter in the old mine, turn to page 300.
To carry on until you reach Ancient Annie's Buffalo Farm, turn to page 263.

As your windy mule lands back on her feet, you head south into the Wilderness, where the landscape is bare and dry. Leafless plants cling to life, snakes hunt on the dusty ground and a faint breeze ruffles your hair, as you ride through the nothingness.

In the near distance, you see a man on horseback. He has a neckerchief pulled over his face and a hat down to his eyebrows. The rider skids to a halt in front of you.

"Gimme your money!" he growls. "And your donkey too!"

"She's not a donkey," you tell him. "She's a mule. And you can't have her, I'm afraid. You see, I'm on a quest to cure the Sheriff's horse."

The man snatches the neckerchief down from his face. He has a scar on his cheek and half his teeth are missing.

"Look, kid, don't you know who I am?" You shrug. You have no idea who he is. You've never been out of Maintown until today. "I'm Billy the Goat, the meanest, baddest, rottenest bandit in the whole of the Wild West. Yee-haw!"

Uh oh. Bandits are dangerous.

You'd better be nice to him.

"Pleased to meet you, Billy the Goat," you reply, a little *too* nicely perhaps. "I don't know your face, but I *do* know your name. You're a very successful bandit, Billy the Goat."

The man sighs.

"I used to be," he replies. "But life's tough out here in the Wilderness. I'm doin' my best to steal an honest livin', but it ain't all ruby rings and gold nuggets. Folk ain't got much to take these days. I mean, look at you, trottin' around the Wild West on the back of a donkey."

"I'm sorry life's hard for you right now, Billy the Goat," you reply. "But if being a bandit is so difficult, why don't you get a job?"

Something lights up in his face. It's as if the idea of getting a job has never occurred to him before.

"A...*job*," muses Billy the Goat, like he's saying the word for the very first time. "Now, there's a thought. But who's gonna hire an ex-bandit?"

"I know the Sheriff of Maintown," you say. "If you tell him I sent you, I'm sure he'll find you something."

The bandit sniffs. Then he takes off his neckerchief to blow his nose.

"Why, that's the kindest thing anyone's ever said to me," he sobs. "I'll go to Maintown right away. Now, tell me, kid, what can Billy the Goat do for you in return?"

"Oh, well, I need some buffalo milk. Do you know where I can find some?"

"Sure do," replies Billy the Goat. "Ancient Annie's Buffalo Farm is just over yonder. Keep walking south 'til you get to Grey Rock, then go around it to reach the farm. The eastern side will take you through Snake Valley, the western side goes via Dead Man's Gorge. Good luck, kid, and thanks for the help," and with that, he gallops north towards Maintown.

And so, as Billy the Goat grows small in the distance, you head over to Grey Rock. Snake Valley is to your right and Dead Man's Gorge is to your left. Both sound like places you'd rather avoid, but which route will you take?

To go through Snake Valley, turn to page 302.
To go via Dead Man's Gorge, turn to page 224.

You throw a rock to get Crabbity Jack's attention. The missile flies over the fence, past the man's head and – *SMASH!* – straight through the side of his greenhouse.

Oopsie!

The old man eyes the shattered glass with a furious look, then glowers over his shoulder before marching towards you with his arms swinging low.

"WHADDA YA RECKON YOU'RE PLAYIN' AT?" he shouts, when he gets to the fence.

"I-I'm sorry," you tell him, "I didn't mean to cause any damage. I was trying to attract your attention."

"CRACKED MY EXTENSION? THAT AIN'T NO EXTENSION, YOU FOOL, THAT'S A GREENHOUSE!"

It seems Crabbity Jack is a little hard of hearing.

"No, I said, I was trying to *attract your attention.*"

"ATTACK MY INVENTION? WHAT INVENTION?"

"No, *attract…your…attention.*"

"YOU AIN'T GONNA EXTRACT NONE O' MY PENSION, YOU CHEEKY YOUNG SCALLYWAG – IT'S *MY* PENSION, NOT YOURS. NOW, GIMME SOME MONEY TO PAY FOR THIS GREENHOUSE."

You have four gold coins in your saddlebag, but they belong to the Sheriff. You're supposed to use them to buy ingredients for the medicine. Should you give them to Crabbity Jack, or explain why he can't have the money?

To give the money to Crabbity Jack, turn to page 254.
To explain why he can't have it, turn to page 278.

You feel a flutter of excitement as you start the long climb to the summit of Purple Mountain. The grassy slopes become rockier the higher up you go and there's a man herding sheep in the distance.

But suddenly, Tumbleweed's legs become wobbly. She's swaying from side to side, staggering up the mountain as if someone just rolled her downhill in an empty barrel.

You climb out of your saddle to investigate.

"There there, old friend," you tell her, patting the top of her furry head, "you'll be all right. Some deep breaths will make you feel better. In through the nose, and out through the mouth, in through the nose, and out through the mouth, in through the nose, and—"

BOOF!

That is the sound of a mule fainting.

You see, the poor creature has been breathing in your terrible stink ever since you left Crabbity Jack's Shack and all those deep breaths have pushed her over the edge. She'll be fine once you've had a wash, but after that you should take her home so she can recover from her ordeal in her nice, comfy, sweet-smelling mule shed.

Never mind, partner. You can use what you've

learnt on your next attempt – just make sure you take a bath first.

Phooey!

Go back to the start of the book to try again, or turn to page 266 to make a different choice.

Wow, your mountain lion impressions are incredible! The jackal is terrified, especially when you swish your imaginary mane and gnash your fake lion-teeth, and he runs away with his tail between his legs.

But it seems your skills were a little *too* good. For suddenly, from behind the skull of a large wildebeest, an *actual* lion appears. He's mistaken you for a member of his pride and runs over to rescue you from the jackal. Of course, when he finds a human being and a tasty mule instead, he eyes the pair of you like a family-size pizza with extra cheese.

Talk about out of the frying pan and into the fire.

Why won't these animals leave you alone?!

How are you going to escape?

To keep doing your lion impression, turn to page 286.
To run to the nearest cactus patch and hide, turn to page 304.

Tumbleweed carries you quietly through the undergrowth towards the nest. It's well-hidden by a branch, so you climb down and part the leaves. The bird's feathers look like the one in Great Grandpappy Pete's drawing, but she's fast asleep and you can't see her legs.

Carefully, you pick up a twig and use it to lift the bird's tail.

SQUAWK! PECK!

Now, here's the thing about birds.

SQUAWK! PECK!

They don't like being poked at with twigs.

SQUAWK! PECK!

No-one likes being poked at with twigs.

SQUAWK! PECK!

Especially not when they're sleeping.

SQUAWK! PECK!

Especially not when they're sitting on a nest full of eggs.

SQUAWK! PECK!

The bird flaps her wings madly and her eyes turn red. They bulge from their sockets like two bright holly berries as she flies into your face, pecking you on the head through a cloud of feathers.

The attack startles your mule. She bucks her hind legs and the saddlebag slides off her back. It lands in the water then floats to the middle of the lake, where a milky white cloud spreads out on the surface as the bag sinks into the weeds.

The little bird alights on a nearby branch and crows happily, as she dances around on her *two* yellow legs.

Gee, partner, that sure is bad luck.

Go back to the start of the book to try again, or turn to page 313 to make a different choice.

Crabbity Jack's Shack is near Purple Mountain. Its lofty peak can be seen from all over the Wild West, so you head towards it on the back of your mule.

After an hour of riding, you reach the western bank of Blue River. There's a large wooden hut on the opposite side – it must be Crabbity Jack's Shack. Next to it, there's a glass greenhouse and a small chicken coop, beyond which a herd of buffalo are grazing on the lush grass. A rickety fence encircles the land, with a wonky gate and a sign you can't read from this side of the river.

You'll need to cross over the water to see what it says. But how?

To make a raft, turn to page 249.
To swim across, turn to page 264.

"That's very kind," you say, "but I have to get on with my quest."

Ancient Annie sighs glumly.

"I understand," she says. "Let's milk a buffalo so you can be on your way."

The old woman shows you across the farm and into the buffalo shed. The floor is covered with straw and there's a hay-bale in the corner. But where are the buffalo?

As you turn to ask Ancient Annie that very question, the door slams and you find yourself alone in a very dark barn.

"Hey, what's going on?" you cry.

The old woman's eyeball peeps through a knot-hole in the wall.

"I ain't seen no-one in a long time, kid, and I do so like a chat. Now, settle down while I tell you *all* about myself…"

The old woman talks for hours.

And hours.

And *hours*.

By nightfall you know every detail of her one-hundred-and-nine years, including the time she married a shepherd on Purple Mountain and had twelve sheep as bridesmaids.

The rodeo will be over by the time you get out of this shed. But you've made a new friend (albeit a rather scary one) and have all the buffalo milk you could ever wish for.

Go back to the start of the book to try again or turn to page 302 to make a different choice.

"Okay," you tell him, "you can take the four coins."

The shepherd snatches them up with glee.

"Ha!" he laughs, handing you the feather. "You've paid *way* too much! So long, sucker!" and he ushers his flock to the other side of the mountain.

That shepherd is a conman.

He has taken advantage of your good nature.

But you've collected *all three* of your ingredients, so who cares? Yee-haw! All you have to do now is go home and make the Itchity Fever medicine in time for the rodeo.

Hurriedly, you look for Maintown on the distant horizon. But you can't see it. You must be standing on the wrong side of Purple Mountain. How will you find your way home?

If you want to climb to the peak of Purple Mountain for a better view of the land, turn to page 218.
If you want to ask Tumbleweed how to get back to Maintown, turn to page 296.

"Yes, please," you say, "that would be lovely."

You tie Tumbleweed to a tree and go into the wooden farmhouse. Ancient Annie makes a fresh pot of tea and serves you a slice of cake. You tell her all about the Sheriff's horse and she tells you all about the time she was a bare-knuckle fighter in Texas City.

When it's time to get on with your quest, the old lady fetches some fresh buffalo milk from her larder. You thank Ancient Annie then step outside to say your goodbyes, where you realise something awful has happened.

Tumbleweed is missing and so are Annie's buffalo!

In the distance, you see a lone horseman riding south. He's towing Tumbleweed on a small trailer and herding Annie's buffalo away from the farm. It's Billy the Goat! He fooled you into thinking he was going to Maintown and turned his hand to rustling instead.

Ancient Annie is furious. She throws you off her farm and you're forced to walk home through Snake Valley alone. Good luck with those serpents, StoryQuester!

Go back to the start of the book to try again, or turn to page 302 to make a different choice.

The Desert of Bones sounds like the kind of place a StoryQuester should go, so you enter the desolate land on the back of your trusty mule.

Phew, it sure is warm here! It's like walking around in an oven with your winter coat on and a hot-water-bottle shoved up your jumper. Your sweaty pong mixes with the smell of buffalo dung to make one giant stink and Tumbleweed is very unhappy. She doesn't like the smell of sweaty buffalo dung, so she kicks her legs in protest and tosses you out of your saddle, before turning tail and trotting back to Maintown.

You can't finish your quest without her, but you can try the Sheriff's challenge again once you've taken a bath.

Go back to the start of the book to try again, or turn to page 266 to make a different choice.

You lean left and the raft travels west along the river. The water here is littered with logs. They're floating in your path like sleeping crocodiles, so you drift carefully in and out of them, taking care not to damage your raft.

Suddenly, one of the logs lifts its head. Then it opens its mouth and shows you its sharp, pointed teeth. Yikes! They're not logs – they really *are* crocodiles!

SNAP!

The first croc almost catches Tumbleweed's tail.

SNAP!

The second tears a hole in your shirt.

SNAP!

And the third just misses your leg as it bites clean through the middle of the raft, leaving you on one half and the mule on the other.

Tumbleweed's side floats to the riverbank, where the old mule saunters onto the bank and disappears into Green Woodland. But the Blue River current takes hold of your portion and carries you through the crocodiles, past the forest and out onto the ocean itself.

Three days later a passing fishing-boat picks you up and ships you back to Maintown, where the Sheriff is mighty relieved you're safe even though you haven't found any ingredients.

Try again soon, partner, and watch out for those crocs!

Go back to the start of the book to try again, or turn to page 249 make a different choice.

As your windy mule lands back on her feet, you head north into the Wilderness.

Tumbleweed trots merrily over the dusty ground, glad to be out of the mule-shed on this beautiful sunny day, when a stagecoach trundles into view. You could ask its passengers if they know where you can find your ingredients.

Hurriedly, you climb out of your saddle and wave your arms in front of the horses. The driver pulls on the reins and the carriage skids to a halt. A large woman in a brown leather suit jumps out. She storms towards you with fury in her eyes, her thick arms swinging at her sides.

There are bears less scary than this on Purple Mountain.

"Dagnabbit!" yells the woman. "I am so darn sick of you thievin' bandits tryin' to hijack my stagecoach! If you want it, you'll have to get through *me* first, or my name ain't Calamity Joan," and she pushes her sleeves up to show you her hairy fists.

Crikey! Calamity Joan is a well-known frontierswoman in these parts. Even the famous bandit, Billy the Goat, is scared of Calamity Joan.

"I-I'm not a thief," you stammer. "I'm just a

stablehand from Maintown. I'm on a quest to cure the Sheriff's horse. Do you know where I can buy some buffalo milk?"

Calamity Joan lowers her fists, but her eyes are still fixed upon yours.

"You could try Crabbity Jack's Shack," she replies. "Ol' Jack keeps a buffalo herd up near Purple Mountain. It's quite a distance to travel by donkey though."

"Oh, she's not a donkey," you tell her. "She's a mule," and you immediately regret having said that.

Calamity Joan curls her top lip.

"Or," she goes on, "you could try the Wilderness Store. It's just over yonder, but there ain't much call for buffalo milk around these parts, so there mightn't be any in stock. Now, get away from my stagecoach, kid, or it'll be fisty-cuffs at dawn," and she climbs back into her carriage.

Where do you want to go next?

If you'd like to go the distance and head over to Crabbity Jack's Shack, turn to page 235.
If you'd rather go to the Wilderness Store, turn to page 315.

You couldn't care less about cactus plants, so you set off through the desert in search of a fresh dragon fruit.

As you trek across the sandy plains, you become aware of a gentle breeze pushing in from the east. It's a welcome break from the scorching heat of the sun, but as the wind grows stronger, it whips at the ground and the air becomes swamped in a haze of orange.

Yikes! A sandstorm!

Tumbleweed can't see where she's going and all she can do is walk aimlessly on in the hope she will find a way out. But when the sand settles many hours later, the cactus patch is still next to you.

You've been travelling in circles for hours and now you're late for the rodeo. Gee, that sucks.

StoryQuest over. Go back to the start of the book to try again.

You take Lightning Bolt into town to surprise the Sheriff, and what a surprise it is.

"Well, bless my boots!" he exclaims. "You've cured my horse of his Itchity Fever! You truly are the best stablehand a Sheriff could wish for! C'mon, partner, let's saddle-up – the rodeo is about to begin!"

This year's celebrations are the greatest you've ever seen. There are people in fancy-dress, a sheep-herding contest, a ragtime band playing your favourite songs, line-dancing groups, yummy food and the most popular riding contest this side of Blue River – the grand barrel-race.

All the best riders have travelled across the Wild West to compete. They saddle-up and gallop around two barrels, in and out of the obstacles as fast as their horses will carry them, and the quickest time wins. But of course, no-one ever beats the Sheriff and that's all part of the fun.

At the end of the competition, Lightning Bolt is awarded a big rosette and the Sheriff tells everyone about his awesome stablehand, who crossed deserts and climbed mountains to save his trusty stead.

A huge cheer goes up as you and Tumbleweed take your place next to the Sheriff.

"I've been thinking," he says, as the crowd go crazy, "a Wild West explorer like you shouldn't be shovelling horse poo for pocket money – how would you like to be my Deputy instead?"

No more poo-shovelling! Yippee!

And later that evening, as the reddening sun sinks into the distant horizon, you walk Tumbleweed back to her shed with your shiny new Deputy's badge twinkling on your hat.

"Gee," you sigh, as your furry friend settles down for the night, "this sure has been a mighty fine adventure."

The mule releases a little wind, and you're pretty sure what she means by that is...

"Yee-haw!"

Congratulations! You've completed your quest and you're going to be the new Deputy Sheriff of Maintown!
If you want to find the ultimate ending to your story, go back to the start of the book and try your adventure again.

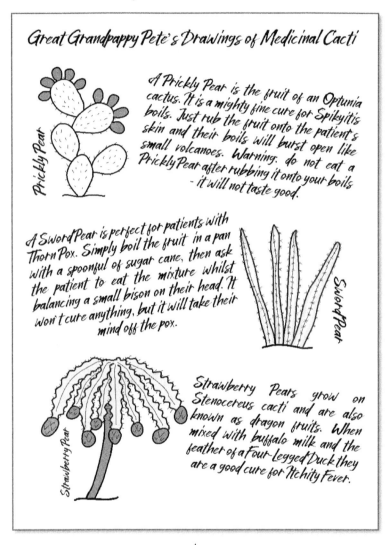

Great Grandpappy Pete's Drawings of Medicinal Cacti

Prickly Pear

A Prickly Pear is the fruit of an Optunia cactus. It is a mighty fine cure for Spikyitis boils. Just rub the fruit onto the patient's skin and their boils will burst open like small volcanoes. Warning: do not eat a Prickly Pear after rubbing it onto your boils - it will not taste good.

A Sword Pear is perfect for patients with Thorn Pox. Simply boil the fruit in a pan with a spoonful of sugar cane, then ask the patient to eat the mixture whilst balancing a small bison on their head. It won't cure anything, but it will take their mind off the pox.

Sword Pear

Strawberry Pear

Strawberry Pears grow on Stenocereus cacti and are also known as dragon fruits. When mixed with buffalo milk and the feather of a Four-Legged Duck they are a good cure for Itchity Fever.

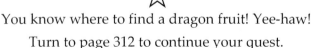

You know where to find a dragon fruit! Yee-haw!

Turn to page 312 to continue your quest.

You gather some sticks to build your raft and lay them out on the riverbank. There's an old lasso in the Sheriff's saddlebag. You use it to tie them together, then push the raft out onto the river.

Tumbleweed steps aboard your makeshift boat. She bobs on the water like a big, hairy duck, then you sit down next to her and let go of the bank.

At once, the current takes hold of your raft and pulls you downstream. You paddle frantically, but the water's heading north and so are you, away from Crabbity Jack's Shack, past the Desert of Bones and on towards Green Woodland.

Cripes, there's a fork in the river!

Lean left to go west, or right to go east!

To lean left, turn to page 241.
To lean right, turn to page 217.

249

Shovelling buffalo poo is very similar to shovelling horse poo, except buffalos are bigger and so is the shovel. It's hard work, but you're an experienced stablehand and soon your job is complete.

Crabbity Jack comes over to inspect your work.

"WHY, YOU'RE THE BEST DARN POO-SHOVELLER THIS SIDE OF GREEN WOODLAND!" he shouts in your face. It's not the greatest compliment you've ever had, but you'll take it. He hands you a pint of his finest buffalo milk. "I RECKON YOU'VE EARNT THIS, KID!"

Yee-haw! You've found your first ingredient and are an incredible human being, but you smell like an elephant's litter-tray after all that shovelling.

Do you want to clean up your act before you search for the other ingredients?

I stink! I'll take a wash in the river. Turn to page 299.

Washing is for wimps! I'll get on with my quest. Turn to page 266.

"It really *is* a Four-Legged Duck feather!" you tell the shepherd. "Here, I have some money in my saddlebag."

You take out the coins and show them to the man.

"WOW, FOUR GOLD COINS!" he exclaims. "I could buy a whole extra flock of sheep with those. Hand 'em over and the feather's yours."

"What, *all* of them?" you gasp. "Four gold coins is a *lot* of money to pay for a feather."

"But this is a very *rare* feather," the shepherd replies. "So either pay up or look somewhere else."

The shepherd wants all four of the Sheriff's gold coins in exchange for one measly feather. What are you going to do?

To give him the four gold coins, turn to page 238.
To make up a sob-story so he lets you buy the feather for a better price, turn to page 295.

You take the StoryQuest Star out of your saddlebag and hand it to the Sheriff.

"You found it!" he cries, his face lighting up with joy. "That sure is mighty fine news, kid! And because you collected the star, there'll be a surprise for you after the barrel-race. But first, let's skedaddle – the rodeo is about to begin!"

This year's celebrations are the greatest you've ever seen. There are people in fancy-dress, a sheep-herding contest, a ragtime band playing your favourite songs, line-dancing groups, yummy food and the most popular riding contest this side of Blue River – the grand barrel-race.

All the best riders have travelled across the Wild West to compete. They saddle-up and gallop around two barrels, in and out of the obstacles as fast as their horses will carry them, and the quickest time wins. But of course, no-one ever beats the Sheriff and that's all part of the fun.

At the end of the competition, the crowd gathers round for the Sheriff's speech.

"Cowgirls and boys," he begins, "I have an announcement to make – this will be my last rodeo as the Sheriff of Maintown. I've decided it's time to retire."

There's a groan of disappointment, but the Sheriff holds up the StoryQuest Star and the people go silent.

"A Sheriff is brave and honest," he says. "And a Sheriff works hard to find the ultimate end to their story, no matter what obstacles stand in their way. Today I set a test, to see if my young stablehand was up to the challenge, and all I can say is... *Yee-haw, partner, you rock!* Cowgirls and boys, let's hear it for the new Sheriff of Maintown!"

The word **SHERIFF** appears on the StoryQuest Star and a cheer goes up as it's pinned to your hat. Then Tumbleweed is rewarded with a frilly rosette and a huge bag of hay.

"This sure has been a mighty fine Wild West adventure," you tell your four-legged friend, as she chomps down her tasty prize, "but I couldn't have done it without you," and as the blazing sun sinks into the distant horizon, a very happy, very windy mule soars across the reddening skyline.

Yee-haw!

Congratulations! You've found the ultimate ending to your StoryQuest adventure and have become the new Sheriff of Maintown! Gee, partner, you're awesome.

You give Crabbity Jack the Sheriff's money. He looks down at the four coins, then back up at you.

"THIS AIN'T ENOUGH TO FIX MY GREENHOUSE!" he shouts. "YOU'LL HAVE TO WORK ON MY FARM TO MAKE UP THE REST! THERE'S A STABLE BEHIND THE SHACK WITH YOUR NAME ON IT AND A WHOLE LOTTA BUFFALO POO THAT NEEDS SHOVELLIN'!"

Oh no, not *more* poo!

This is going to take you all day!

That evening you return to Maintown with no ingredients and the Sheriff docks your wages until you've paid back all of his coins. But don't worry, StoryQuester – you can use what you've learnt to complete the Sheriff's challenge on your next attempt.

Yee-haw!

Go back to the start of the book to try again, or turn to page 228 to make a different choice.

You run from the alligator and start the long climb to the top of Purple Mountain, imagining all the fearsome creatures who might live on these slopes: eagles the size of dragons, wolves with teeth like daggers and bears with razor-sharp claws. But never in your worst nightmare did you think you would face the hideous beast that now crosses your path.

Its teeth are gruesomely wonky, its ears are repulsively floppy, its tail is horrendously cute and its voice sounds like the call of a startled sheep.

"MEHHHHHHHHHHHHHHHHHH!"

Buckle up, partner, you've been seen by a *goat!*

The creature stares at you through bulging eyes (well, through *one* bulging eye – the other one's swivelling around in its socket with a life of its own). He lowers his head and scuffs a back foot on the grass. He'll butt you all the way back to Maintown if you don't do something!

I'll tell him to clear off and get on with my quest. Turn to page 280.

Goats are scary – I'm running away to the Desert of Bones. Turn to page 273.

"HELP!" you shout at the top of your lungs, as you bounce along on your raft.

But what you don't realise is the ears of a mule are highly sensitive. They're *so* sensitive in fact that if you stand in the middle of London and talk to a mule in New York, she will hear what you're saying and most likely release a little wind in response. So when you bellow the word, "HELP!" right next to Tumbleweed's ear, she almost jumps out of her skin and immediately comes up with a plan to shut you up.

The old mule snatches a jawful hay from the saddlebag. She shoves it into your mouth, where it blocks your noise-hole like a big ball of hair down a gargling drain and the rocking of the water makes you swallow it whole.

GULP!

A gurgling, rumbling, grumbling sound grows inside your tummy, and then...

PAAARRRRRRRRRRRRRRRP!

The wind hits the water like a typhoon and propels the raft back upstream, through the rapids, between the trees of Green Woodland, past the fork in the river and along the side of the desert, before finally coming to a stand-still directly opposite Crabbity Jack's Shack.

It looks like Tumbleweed isn't the only one who gets windy from eating hay.

Hurriedly, you climb off the raft to help your mule onto the bank. You see the fence encircling the small patch of farmland. The sign reads, CRABBITY JACK'S FARM - BEWARE OF THE DOGS and there's a man in the distance wearing a big straw hat. He's collecting eggs from a chicken coop. He must be Crabbity Jack.

"Howdy!" you call out. "I'm looking for some buffalo milk!"

But the man doesn't hear you.

What do you want to do?

To ignore the warning sign and open the gate, turn to page 290.

To throw a rock and attract the farmer's attention, turn to page 228.

Great Grandpappy Pete's Drawings of Medicinal Birds

The eggs of the Many-Eyed Goose are a good cure for the Sniffles. Just pop the eggs up the patient's nostrils and the problem will go away. If the treatment fails, the doctor should whisk the egg until light and fluffy, then cook over a medium heat for three minutes. It won't cure the Sniffles, but it will make a mighty fine omelette.

The beak of a Needle-Nosed Crow can be useful for cleaning a patient's teeth. Stand the bird on their face and let it hammer away at the plaque with its big, sharp, pointy beak. Patients don't like this method of tooth-cleaning, but if it's good enough for crocodiles, it's good enough for them.

The feather of a Four-Legged Duck can cure a patient's Itchity Fever. It is also good for the Wiggly Woos, the Squirmy Wirmies and the Wriggly Jigglies. Four-legged Ducks are notoriously hard to find, but are mostly found in the strs of m nt

☆

There's mud on the writing, but it seems to say 'streets of Maintown'. Yee-haw! Turn to page 287.

With a clippity-clop and a cloppity-clip, you trot through town on the back of your mule. Tumbleweed is a friendly creature, but a little timid. You want her to know she can trust you and the best way to do that is through her stomach.

Reaching down into your saddlebag, you take out a handful of hay. The mule chomps it down eagerly, and as she chews, a rumbling, grumbling, gargling sound grows in her stomach, until…

PAARRRRRRRRRRRRRRRRP!

Wowsers! The Sheriff wasn't joking when he said hay makes Tumbleweed windy! The mule's bottom sends the pair of you shooting up into the sky like a big, hairy firework, where you gaze out at the vast Wilderness surrounding your town. It's a desolate land roamed by robbers and bandits (and goats), which is why you've never ventured out of Maintown before.

Which way will you enter the Wilderness when you come back to earth? Take a look at Great Grandpappy Pete's map in the back of this book to decide.

To travel north, turn to page 243.
To travel south, turn to page 225.

"Quick, Tumbleweed, scarper!" you shout, and the mule runs past the shepherd to continue up Purple Mountain.

The higher you go, the thinner the air. It's difficult to breathe at such a great height, so you stop for a rest in the shade of a tree. Your head is spinning, your eyelids are heavy, and suddenly the world goes black...

When you wake up, you're lying on the floor of Lightning Bolt's stable with the Sheriff by your side.

"Howdy," he smiles, softly.

"What happened?" you ask.

"You spent too long on the top of Purple Mountain and fainted," the Sheriff explains. "But Tumbleweed carried you home. I reckon you've got a real pal for life there, kid."

Gee, StoryQuester, those sure are tough beans to swallow – but with a friend like Tumbleweed, you're sure to complete the Sheriff's challenge once you're feeling better.

Go back to the start of the book to try again, or turn to page 274 to make different choice.

There's no time to waste at the store, so you run into the stable and grab a mucking-out bucket. You pour in the buffalo milk, squeeze the juice out of the dragon fruit and drop in the Four-Legged Duck feather.

At once, something wonderful happens. Little multicoloured bubbles rise to the surface of the mixture. They float up out of the bucket and then burst into tiny rainbows, each one falling back into the medicine like blossom as the feather crumbles into a sparkling, golden dust.

Your Itchity Fever medicine is ready!

Quickly, you run outside to the paddock with your bucket. The Sheriff's horse is itching himself on a tree, but with a little encouragement you persuade him to taste the mixture. He likes it. In fact, he likes it *so* much that he drinks the whole bucketful and burps out the biggest rainbow you've ever seen.

BAAAAAAAAAAAAAARP!

A beautiful arc of colours stretches out across the Wild West and the Sheriff's horse immediately stops wriggling.

You've cured Lightning Bolt of his Itchity Fever and are the most magnificent StoryQuester that ever lived! But will you tell the Sheriff *before the rodeo,* or surprise him at the barrel-race?

To go to the Sheriff's house, turn to page 292.
To take Lightning Bolt straight to the rodeo and surprise him, turn to page 246.

As you trek on towards Ancient Annie's Buffalo Farm, the blazing sun shines white in the cloudless sky. The heat is intense. Poor Tumbleweed is walking slower, and slower, but suddenly she turns tail and dashes towards Grey Rock.

Its shadow offers her a cool shade to lie down in and she won't leave until the sun drops below the horizon.

Oh, pants! Your mule has overheated and you can't carry on with your quest. Keep cool on your next attempt if you want to find that buffalo milk, partner.

Go back to the start of the book to try again, or turn to page 224 to make a different choice.

You take off your shoes and sit on the bank, hoping no alligators are lurking in the depths of Blue River.

Brrr! The water's freezing despite the warmth of the sun, but as you lower yourself in you discover the river is much shallower than it looks – the water stops at your knees! Phew!

You lead Tumbleweed into the river and wade across to the other side, where you read the sign on the wonky gate:

CRABBITY JACK'S SHACK - BEWARE OF THE DOGS

You can't see any dogs, but you *can* see an old man collecting eggs from a chicken coop. He must be Crabbity Jack.

"Howdy!" you call out. "I'm looking for some buffalo milk!"

But the man doesn't hear you. What do you want to do?

To ignore the warning sign and open the gate, turn to page 290.

To throw a rock and attract Crabbity Jack's attention, turn to page 228.

You lean forward in your saddle to feed Tumbleweed a handful of hay.

CHOMP, CHOMP, CHOMP…

The jackal lowers its head. You'll never outrun it, there's no point in trying, so you close your eyes, hold onto your breath and prepare for the worst, when…

PAARRRRRRRRRRRRRRRP!

A big gust of wind shoots out of the mule. It sends you both flying across the desert like a giant deflating balloon, leaving the jackal in a cloud of sand.

Yee-haw!

Good old Tumbleweed!

You come to a standstill near a big patch of cactus plants. There's a little pool a short distance away, with a flat rock to sit on and a tree with green coconuts. You know it's a mirage and it isn't really there. So why do you feel drawn to it like a cowboy to a new pair of pointy-toed boots with frills down the sides?

To go to the mirage, turn to page 268.

To investigate the cactus patch, turn to page 270.

Washing is for wimps, so you stay smelly and carry on with your challenge. After all, it's only you and the mule on this quest, and you don't suppose Tumbleweed will mind you being a bit whiffy.

You decide to search for the dragon fruit next, but you have no idea where to find one. You'll have to choose a direction and hope for the best. Go south to climb Purple Mountain, or west to explore the Desert of Bones.

The choice is yours, mighty StoryQuester!

Let's climb Purple Mountain! Turn to page 230.
The Desert of Bones sounds good! Turn to page 240.

You throw Tumbleweed at the bank so she doesn't fall into the water, and, well, it's a nice idea, but Tumbleweed is a mule. A very big, very heavy mule. Plus, you're standing on a raft in the middle of a river. It would be hard to lift an eyebrow out here, let alone a mule.

And so, as your attempt at throwing a mule fails, Tumbleweed plummets into the raging water like a big, hairy boulder.

"TUMBLEWEEEEEEEEEEEEED!" you cry.

Luckily, Blue River isn't as deep as it looks. The water barely covers Tumbleweed's knees, so she wades to safety as you and your raft drift further downstream. She will have wandered off by the time you get back to her, so your StoryQuest is over. Maybe try throwing something smaller next time, like a squirrel.

Go back to the start of the book to try again, or turn to page 217 to make a different choice. Also, please don't *actually* throw squirrels – they'll go nuts.

You tie Tumbleweed to a cactus and walk to the mirage. The pool looks so real you can see your reflection in it and a gentle breeze ripples the surface. But when you dip your hand in the clear water, something incredible happens.

Suddenly, the ground next to you swirls into a deep whirlpool and a pillar of sand grows out of the hole. It towers over you, spinning in a blur of orange, before forming the shape of a woman.

She blinks down at you through pearly eyes.

"You have *got* to be kidding me," she snorts. "Not *another* desert. Which one is it this time?"

"The, erm, Desert of Bones," you reply, timidly.

"What a cheery little name," says the woman. "Oh well, seeing as you've kindly summoned me into this *snake-pit* by sticking your hand in that imaginary pool, I suppose I should do my big intro." The sand-woman clears her throat. "BEHOLD, I AM QUEEN SANDRA, IMMORTAL RULER OF SAND!"

"Ruler of…*sand?*" you say, trying not to laugh.

"Yes, you know, those little grains of eroded rocks that get stuck in uncomfortable places when you go to the beach. Not that I'd know. No-one ever summons me to a beach. I don't suppose people need the help of an immortal being when they're sunning themselves in Barbados. No, it's all deserts and egg-timers for me. Anyway, what sand-related problem can I help with today?"

"Oh, well, I'm on a quest to—"

"Say no more," says the woman. "I might've known there was a quest involved. You'd better take this."

A golden star materialises in her hand. The sunlight catches it and the number 252 glistens on one side.

"A StoryQuest Star!" you cry. "Wow, thank you!"

"No time for all that," she replies. "Just listen up so I can leave this litter-tray and get back to my immortal plain. You must memorise the number on the StoryQuest Star, then visit the Sheriff *before the rodeo*. When you hand him the star, you'll unlock the ultimate end to your story. Oh, and do me a favour – next time you go on a quest, do it in Hawaii," and as you tuck the star safely into your pocket, Queen Sandra crumbles back into the desert and the mirage disappears.

Congratulations – you've found the StoryQuest Star!
Turn to page 270 to go back to the cactus patch and continue your quest.

The cactus patch is full of, well, cactus plants. In fact, there are more types of cactus here than you even knew existed. There are thin ones, fat ones, tall ones, short ones, ones with flowers, ones with hair, and one that looks like Mrs Bullwinkle from the Maintown Store.

If you'd like to learn more about cactus plants, you should check out Great Grandpappy Pete's notebook.

I love cactus plants – let's read the notebook. Turn to page 248.

I couldn't care less about cactus plants – let's not. Turn to page 245.

"I'm sorry," you say, "that's not true at all. I thought four gold coins was an unfair price to pay for a feather, so I lied," and you hang your head in shame.

But to your surprise, the shepherd holds out the feather.

"Here," he says. "It takes courage to admit you've done wrong, kid, so I reckon you deserve this free of charge."

You're speechless. Honesty really *is* the best policy! Yee-haw! And now you have your final ingredient, all that's left to do is get back to Maintown in time for the rodeo.

Thanking the shepherd, you search for your town on the landscape below. But you can't see it. You must be on the wrong side of Purple Mountain. How will you find your way home?

To climb higher up Purple Mountain for a better view of the land, turn to page 218.

To ask Tumbleweed to find the way home, turn to page 276.

You show Tumbleweed out of the Wilderness Store then go back inside to ask the storekeeper for a pint of buffalo milk.

She places a bottle of yellow gunk on the counter.

It has a whiff of public toilets about it.

"Are you sure this buffalo milk's fresh?" you ask.

"Sure is," she says. "It was fresh from the udder the day I got it. And that was only four months ago."

Four months?! In years to come, scientists will discover new life-forms in that bottle and use them to cure the most awful diseases. But for now, it's just a pint of gone-off milk.

Politely, you tell the storekeeper you've changed your mind and leave. But when you step outside, you realise something terrible has happened – Tumbleweed has gone! You see, mules have a habit of wandering off, so you can't leave them alone without securing them to a tree or a post. But don't worry, StoryQuester – you can use what you've learnt about mules to save the Sheriff's horse on your next attempt.

Go back to the start of the book to try again, or turn to page 315 to make a different choice.

You and your mule make a dash for safety as the creature starts to attack. You run and you run, and you don't look back, until finally reaching the hot sandy plains of the desert.

Phew! It looks like you lost him!

The Desert of Bones is an eerie place, littered with skeletons and skulls. From the corner of your eye, you see a wolf-like creature stalking across the sand. It's a jackal, a very hungry jackal, and its eyes are fixed upon *you*. The Wild West is crawling with dangerous animals, but jackals are a particularly cunning species. You'll have to think fast if you want to outwit this wily predator.

What's the plan, partner?

To pretend you're a mountain lion and scare the jackal away, turn to page 232.

To feed Tumbleweed some hay to calm her nerves, turn to page 265.

273

You cross the river and head east onto the rocky slopes of Purple Mountain. From halfway up, you see a huge flock of birds swarming above you. Some have big wings, some have little wings, some have long legs, some have short legs, some have beaks, some don't have beaks (no, wait, those are squirrels) and they're all cawing and crowing and squawking their heads off.

Suddenly, you meet a man herding sheep.

"Howdy," you say. The shepherd doffs his hat. "I'm on a quest to cure the Sheriff's horse and I'm looking for a special feather. Do you know where I might find a Four-Legged Duck?"

"Haw, haw, haw!" laughs the shepherd. "You'll be lucky, kiddo. No-one's seen a Four-Legged Duck around here for ages. Although..." From the rim of his hat, he takes a feather. It has black and white stripes with a long, pointed tip. "I did find *this* a few years back."

"Crikey!" you gasp. "Is it—"

"Yup, that's the tail feather of a Four-Legged Duck all right."

"How do you know?"

"Listen, partner, I've lived and worked on these slopes for forty-five years. Heck, I even got married on 'em once. I know every feather of every bird and this one came from a Four-Legged Duck. You can have it for a price. Have you got any gold?"

Is this guy for real? Does he *actually* have the tail feather of a Four-Legged Duck, or is he just after your money?

I think he's a bandit in disguise – let's scarper! Turn to page 260.

I'll read Great Grandpappy Pete's notebook to see if the feather is genuine. Turn to page 221.

You lean forward to whisper in Tumbleweed's ear.

"Listen," you say, "I know you're a mule and all that, but if you understand what I'm saying, please could you take me back to Maintown?"

The mule's ears twitch. Then she scuffs the ground with her hoof. Did she understand what you said? Or has she got wind again? And then...

WHOOSH!

That's not wind! *That* is the sound of a mule who's never been asked anything so politely in her whole entire life, speeding down the side of a mountain like a champion racehorse. You see, Tumbleweed knows *exactly* how to get home. She's a mule, and mules have an excellent sense of direction. She's basically a big, hairy compass on legs.

Before long, you're galloping past Crabbity Jack's Shack, across Blue River, through the Desert of Bones and into the Wilderness, where a small town appears in the distance.

Maintown!

Yee-haw!

It looks like the rodeo is about to start. Banners and flags have been strewn between the buildings, and the streets are lined with cowgirls and boys from all over the Wild West. And on the outskirts of town, a lady is charging visitors a fee to get in.

"Howdy," she smiles, as you climb out of your saddle. "Welcome to the Maintown Rodeo. That'll be three gold coins, please," and she holds out her hand for your payment.

Phew! It's lucky you didn't give all your money to that swindling shepherd!

Hurriedly, you hand over the coins and ride to the Sheriff's stables. Lightning Bolt is still scratching himself on a fencepost in the paddock. You're running out of time – you'd better make the medicine and fast.

But what will you mix the ingredients in?

To use a mucking-out bucket from the stable, turn to page 261.

To buy a bowl from Mrs Bullwinkle at the Maintown Store, turn to page 222.

"I'm sorry," you tell Crabbity Jack, "but I can't give you that money. It belongs to the Sheriff of Maintown."

"THE FERRET OF BRAINTOWN?" scowls the old man. "WHAT'RE YOU TALKIN' ABOUT? LOOK, KID, WHEN FOLK DAMAGE OTHER PEOPLE'S PROPERTY, THEY PAY TO MEND IT AND THAT'S THE RULE."

"I can pay you tomorrow," you tell him, "with my own money. I don't want to break the rule, but—"

"TAKE THE MULE?"

"No, that's not what I said. I said, I don't want to *break the rule.*"

"I SUPPOSE I *COULD* TAKE THE MULE INSTEAD OF A PAYMENT."

"That's not what I said! I said, *break the rule, BREAK THE RULE!*"

"ALL RIGHT, ALL RIGHT, NO NEED TO KEEP GOING ON ABOUT IT!" Crabbity Jack takes hold of Tumbleweed's reins and leads her onto his farm. "THERE, I'VE TAKEN THE MULE. NOW GET OFF MY LAND, YOU LITTLE VANDAL, AND DON'T COME BACK!"

You've lost your mule to Crabbity Jack, but you

were *so* close to finding that buffalo milk. Good luck on your next attempt, StoryQuester!

Go back to the start of the book to try again, or turn to page 228 to make a different choice.

"Hey, goat!" you shout, climbing down from your mule. "I'm not scared of you and your spinning eyeball! Leave us alone, or I'll...I'll...I'll shoo you away!"

The goat doesn't care. In fact, he looks even angrier now than he did before.

"*MEEHHHHHHHH!*"

"Right, that's it," you say. "Here it comes. *SHOO!*"

Your voice is like a red flag to a bull. The goat lowers his horns, snorts fiercely then charges towards you, butting you so hard you soar into the air and land on the very top of Purple Mountain.

Gee, the goats of the Wild West sure are strong!

You look down from your lofty perch. Tumbleweed is already making her way back to Maintown and you wish you were going with her. But the rocks here are too steep to climb, so you stay on the summit all night, listening to the taunting cries of the goats pushing up through the darkness below.

"*MEEHHHHHHHH!*"

Go back to the start of the book to try again, or turn to page 255 to make a different choice.

You approach the hermit to ask about Four-Legged Ducks.

"Excuse me, sir. I'm sorry to bother you, but—"

"I know what you're thinking," the man interrupts. He has a posh British accent and a piece of grass stuck between his two front teeth. "You're wondering where you know me from, aren't you?" (You're not. You thought he was a hermit.) "It's me! Horatio Smythe, famous scientist and all-round good egg." (He doesn't look like a scientist. Or an egg.) "My colleague and I, Professor Rogers, have been living here in Green Woodland for the last two years. We're studying the wildlife. The Professor just popped out to investigate some Silver-Feathered Goose chicks down on the lake. Would you like my autograph?"

"Erm, that's okay," you reply. "I just wondered if you've seen any Four-Legged Ducks?"

"Four-Legged Ducks, eh?" muses Horatio Smythe. "Those are mountain birds – you won't find any down here. Are you sure you don't want my autograph? I could sign your mule."

You can't tell if Horatio Smythe really is a scientist, or if he's a wagon-wheel short of a stagecoach. So as the scruffy man searches his tent for a pen, you decide to check Great Grandpappy Pete's notebook to see if he's right about Four-Legged Ducks.

Quickly, you take the item out of your saddlebag and flick through the pages. But in your hurry, the book slips through your fingers and falls onto the muddy ground.

Oh, dear. Some of the pages are dirty and smudged. Do you still want to check Great Grandpappy Pete's notes, or will you trust Horatio Smythe and go straight to Purple Mountain?

To trust Horatio Smythe and go straight to Purple Mountain, turn to page 274.
To check Great Grandpappy Pete's muddy notes, turn to page 258.

You've had enough poo-shovelling to last you a lifetime, so you offer to shear Crabbity Jack's sheep instead.

His flock are grazing uphill from the shack. It's windy on this side of the building and as you walk towards the field a sudden breeze blows a spattering of grit into your eyes.

Ouch!

It stings like salt and you can't blink it out. But there's a job to be done, so you carefully take hold of the nearest sheep and start shearing. A pile of wool forms on the grass, then Crabbity Jack comes out of his shack to inspect your handiwork. He's carrying a bottle of buffalo milk and he looks pleased with your sheep-shearing efforts.

Until suddenly, he stops.

He squints across the field.

His nostrils flare like a cowboy's jeans and his jaw drops to his chest.

"*ROVER!*" he cries. "*MY DEAR ROVER!*"

Rover? That's a weird name for a sheep.

With a hard blink, the grit finally leaves your eyes, your vision clears and...

Argh! That's not a sheep! It's a dog! It's a bald dog

standing next to a big pile of hair! You've accidentally shaved Crabbity Jack's dog and you can't make a jumper out of dog hair! Well, you probably *could* but you definitely shouldn't.

What are you going to do?

To offer Crabbity Jack some money, turn to page 307.

To grab the milk and leg-it, turn to page 289.

Great Grandpappy Pete's Drawings of Medicinal Feathers

The feather of a Long-Nosed Peacock is good for patients who are being sat on by a horse. A doctor should use the feather to tickle the animal under its armpit or on the foot. This will make the horse giggle so much it will fall off the patient. Please note, finding the armpit of an animal without arms can often prove tricky.

The feather of a Sabre-Toothed Robin is an excellent treatment for patients who are stuck in the swing-door of a saloon. The medically trained person should drop the feather near the patient, shouting, "Argh! A Sabre-Toothed Robin! We're all goners!" and the patient will immediately unstick themselves from the door and run off down the street.

The feather of a Four-Legged Duck is known for its use on patients who prickle themselves on a cactus. It can be mixed with a pint of buffalo milk and the juice of a fresh dragon fruit and used as an effective cure for Itchity Fever.

Yee-haw! You've learnt that a Four-Legged Duck's feather is stripy! Turn to page 313 to continue with your quest.

You continue your lion impression by showing your teeth and snarling fiercely.

"RARGH!"

The real mountain lion looks at you with interest. He pads towards you. Then he sniffs your face and his eyes soften. He thinks you're his long-lost cub, the same cub who wandered into the Wilderness one day and never returned. He hasn't seen you for years, but now you're back and soon to be reunited with the pride.

Ah, it's a Wild West *miracle.*

Of course, it's actually no miracle at all. You're just *really* good at animal impressions. But you can't argue with a mountain lion, so you follow him to Purple Mountain where you change your name to Rory and live as one of the pride for the rest of your days. It's not a bad life, here in the den. But the vegetarian options are limited.

Go back to the start of the book to try again, or turn to page 232 to make a different choice.

Great Grandpappy Pete says you can find a Four-Legged Duck on the streets of Maintown, so you thank Horatio Smythe for his help (even though he was no help at all) and steer Tumbleweed towards Blue River. From there, you go through the desert, across the Wilderness and back to Maintown, where the rodeo preparations are well underway.

Banners and flags have been hung between buildings, people are practising their horse-riding skills and there are tables full of delicious snacks outside the local saloon. And amongst it all, the Sheriff is pacing the street with worry.

"Howdy, partner!" he cries, as he sees you enter the town. "Have you found everythin' we need for Lightnin' Bolt's medicine?"

"Almost," you reply. "I have the buffalo milk and a fresh dragon fruit. And according to Great Grandpappy Pete's notebook, I can find a Four-Legged Duck right here on the streets of Maintown."

The Sheriff frowns.

"Really?" he says. "I've lived in Maintown my whole life and I ain't never seen no Four-Legged Ducks. Gimme a look at those notes, kid."

You hand the Sheriff his grandfather's book.

"The page is muddy," he says, "but I'm pretty sure that says Four-Legged Ducks can be found in the *streams of mountains*.'"

"Oh, no!" you cry. "You're right, and so was Horatio Smythe! Four-Legged ducks really *do* live on Purple Mountain!"

"Horatio Smythe?" frowns the Sheriff. "You mean the world famous scientist and all round good-egg? Did you get his autograph?"

The rodeo is about to begin and you don't have time to go back out of town. But well done for finding two ingredients, partner! Yee-haw!

Go back to the start of the book to try again, or turn to page 281 to make a different choice.

You grab the bottle of milk from Crabbity Jack and run towards the gate. It's a bad idea. For a start, thieves never prosper. And for another, Crabbity Jack might be old, but, wow, is he fast.

The aging farmer chases after you like an angry bull, shouting naughty words and swinging a spade over his head. You panic and speed up your pace, catching a foot on the uneven ground in your hurry and – whoosh! – up you go, soaring into the air like an arrow, over the sheep, past the buffalo and straight through the roof of a small chicken coop.

KERASH!

Crabbity Jack comes storming across the field.

"YOU THIEVIN' SCOUNDREL!" yells the farmer. "I'M TAKIN' YOUR MULE AS PAYMENT FOR THAT BUFFALO MILK, NOT TO MENTION THOSE EGGS YOU'VE BROKEN! NOW GET OFF MY LAND BEFORE I THROW YOU OFF!"

Go back to the start of the book to try again, or turn to page 283 to make a different choice.

You ignore the sign saying, CRABBITY JACK'S SHACK – BEWARE OF THE DOGS and open the gate.

The rusty hinge creaks as you step onto Crabbity Jack's land. It acts as an alarm and a huge pack of dogs immediately bursts out of the shack.

"WOOF! WOOF! WOOF! WOOF! WOOF!"

There are at least thirty of them, maybe more, and they're running towards you on thundering paws like one big, hairy monster. Before you know it they've knocked you over and pinned you down on the grass.

But they're not snarling or growling, they're not biting or snapping. And then you realise – these aren't guard-dogs, they're a big happy family of Golden Retrievers.

You laugh at the dogs' funny open-mouthed smiles, as they dance around with their tongues hanging out, wagging their tails and licking you on the face. Crabbity Jack hears the commotion. He spins around and glares at you through a monobrow the size of a young sheep. He has a face like a leather saddlebag and ears like two rashers of crispy bacon.

"WHAT'S ALL THE NOISE?" he shouts. Then he marches over and stares down at you. "WHO ARE YOU AND WHADDA YOU WANT?"

"Sorry to disturb you, sir," you say, jumping to your feet. "I'm on a quest to cure the Sheriff's horse and I'm looking for a pint of buffalo milk."

Crabbity Jack's rubbery forehead folds into his hat like a concertina.

"BUNGALOW SILK? WHAT'S THAT?"

"No, I said, *buffalo milk*."

"DOMINO STILTS?"

"No, *buffalo milk*."

"A TOMATO KILT?"

It seems Crabbity Jack is a little hard of hearing.

"No, sir, I'm looking for some *buffalo milk*."

"OH, BUFFALO MILK!" he replies. "WHY DIDN'T YOU SAY SO? I GOT PLENTY – IF YOU LEND A HAND ON MY FARM, I'LL FETCH YOU A PINT. YOU CAN EITHER SHEAR A FEW SHEEP, OR SHOVEL SOME BUFFALO DUNG. WHICH IS IT TO BE?"

Pass me the shovel! Turn to page 250.

I'd rather try my hand at sheep-shearing. Turn to page 283.

You trot to the Sheriff's house to tell him you've cured Lightning Bolt of his Itchity Fever.

"Well, bless my boots!" he exclaims. "That sure is the finest darn thing I ever did hear. You should be mighty proud of yourself, partner! I'd love to hear all about your Wild West adventures, but first things first – do you have the StoryQuest Star for me?"

If you collected the StoryQuest Star from Queen Sandra, turn to the page number you saw glittering on the object when she handed it over.
If you don't have the star, don't worry, you're still awesome! Turn to page 310.

"Of course I'm telling the truth," you reply. "Do you think I'd lie about a poor, sick little puppy?"

The shepherd puts the Four-Legged Duck Feather back into the rim of his hat.

"You can't pull the wool over a shepherd's eyes," he says. "I can tell when folk are lying. You keep your coins, and I'll keep my feather. Good luck with your quest, kid," and with that, he ushers his flock to the other side of the mountain.

Oh, dear. The shepherd has seen right through you and you have to start your feather-hunt all over again. But after searching the rocky slopes of Purple Mountain for the next three hours, when darkness falls you're forced to head back to Maintown without your final ingredient.

Go back to the start of the book to try again, or turn to page 295 to make a different choice.

You pick up an animal bone and part the leaves of the prickly plant. Then you reach through, take hold of the dragon fruit and with a gentle snap it leaves the cactus.

Congratulations!

You've collected your second ingredient!

Yee-haw!

All you need now is the feather of a Four-Legged Duck and your quest is complete.

But you won't find any ducks here in the desert, it's far too dry. The Sheriff's divination stick could show you where to find water, or you could try looking in the babbling streams of Purple Mountain.

Which would you like to do?

To look on Purple Mountain, turn to page 274.

To use the divination stick, turn to page 215.

You decide to make up a sob-story, one that's sad enough to convince the shepherd to part with his feather for a better price.

"I can't give you all four of my coins," you tell him, "because I need the rest to buy food for my poor, sick little puppy."

Everyone loves a puppy, right?

"Well, I wouldn't want a sick puppy to go hungry," the shepherd replies. "Okay, if you swear you're telling the truth, you can buy the feather for one gold coin."

Well, this is yee-h*awkward*. Are you going to tell the truth, or carry on with your lie?

To reply, "Of course I'm telling the truth," turn to page 293.

To own-up and admit it's a lie, turn to page 271.

You lean forward to whisper in Tumbleweed's ear.

"Listen," you say, "I know you're a mule and all that, but if you understand what I'm saying, please could you take me back to Maintown?"

The mule's ears twitch. She scuffs the ground with her hoof. Did she understand what you said? Or has she got wind again? And then...

WHOOSH!

That's not wind. *That* is the sound of a mule who's never been asked to do anything so politely in her whole entire life, speeding down the side of a mountain like a champion racehorse. You see, Tumbleweed knows *exactly* how to get home. She's a mule, and mules have an excellent sense of direction. She's basically a big, hairy compass on legs.

Before long, you're galloping past Crabbity Jack's Shack, across Blue River, through the desert and into the Wilderness, where a small town appears in the distance.

Maintown! Yee-haw!

It looks like the rodeo is about to start. Banners and flags have been strewn between the buildings, and the streets are lined with cowgirls and boys from all over the Wild West. And on the outskirts of town, a lady is charging visitors a fee to get in.

"Howdy," she smiles. "Welcome to the Maintown Rodeo. That'll be three gold coins, please," and she holds out her hand for your payment.

Dagnabbit! You don't have any coins. You gave them all to the shepherd on Purple Mountain. But what you *do* have is a plan.

Quickly, you take out the buffalo milk, the dragon fruit and the Four-Legged Duck feather.

"I can't pay to get into Maintown," you tell the woman, "but the Sheriff urgently needs these ingredients. Can you make sure he gets them, please?"

The woman snorts.

"Does this *look* like a delivery service?" she asks. "If you ain't got no money, kid, just clear off."

You thought this might happen, it's all part of the plan, so you feed Tumbleweed the tiniest piece of hay and…

PARP.

The woman scowls. Her face turns green. Then her eyes bulge and her nose wiggles.

"All right, all right!" she cries. "I'll make sure the Sheriff gets the ingredients! Just take your windy mule and get outta here before everyone leaves town!"

Good old Tumbleweed has saved the day!

And later that evening, once the rodeo has

finished, you return to Maintown to walk your mule back to her shed. The Sheriff is still clearing up outside the ol' saloon.

"*There* you are!" he exclaims. "I was wonderin' where you'd got to. Thanks for sendin' me those ingredients, partner – you sure are the best stablehand a Sheriff could wish for. I mixed the medicine in time for the barrel-race and Lightnin' Bolt won first prize. But we ain't the ones who did all the hard work, so I reckon it's *you* who deserves this."

He hands you a big golden trophy.

"Wow!" you smile. "Thanks, Sheriff! But I couldn't have done it without Tumbleweed."

The man's moustache gives an impish twitch.

"Sure thing," he replies. "Which is why I've put some extra hay in her shed tonight," and as the blazing sun sinks into the distant horizon, a very happy, very windy mule zips across the skyline like a hairy shooting-star.

Yee-haw!

Congratulations! You've completed the challenge and cured the Sheriff's horse!
If you want to find the ultimate ending, go back to the start of the book and try again.

A wash in Blue River is just what you need and it certainly makes you smell better.

But when you climb out of the water, you're followed by a long, green alligator. Two pointed teeth hang over its bottom lip and its huge tail lashes the ground like a whip as it stalks towards you.

Uh oh. The alligators of the Wild West are almost as dangerous as the goats. You'd better get out of here fast. Where will you run to?

To head for Purple Mountain, turn to page 255.
To go to the Desert of Bones, turn to page 273.

You shelter from the sun in the disused gold mine. It's much cooler in here and Tumbleweed is glad of the shade. But suddenly, there's a noise in the darkness. A man wearing scruffy clothes walks in from an adjoining room.

"Howdy," he says. "What're you doing in Dead Man's Gorge?"

"I'm on a quest to cure the Sheriff's horse," you reply. "Do you work here?"

"Sure do," says the man. "The name's Stanley Miner. I've worked here for more than eighty years and I've only been dead for twelve of 'em."

GASP!

"You mean you're a g-g-g-ghost?"

"That's right," he says. "But there ain't no need for all that stuttering. Folk weren't scared of me when I was alive, so they shouldn't be scared of me now. This is my gorge, partner, and you'll always be welcome here."

Two animal ghosts materialise through the far wall. One is a horse and the other's a donkey. Tumbleweed looks curiously at the pair. Then she trots over and the three of them rub noses.

"Well, blow me down with a stick of dynamite,"

300

breathes Stanley Miner. "Tumbleweed, is that you?"

The mule releases a little wind.

PARP.

"It *is* you!" cries the ghost. He floats over to join the animals. "These two are Tumbleweed's parents," he explains. "They were working in the mine when she was born, but the Sheriff of Maintown rescued her when she was a foal. He gave her a much better life than she woulda had here." Stanley Miner strokes Tumbleweed's head like a long-lost relative. "How's life treating you, old pal?"

Tumbleweed is so happy to see her family again you don't have the heart to leave. So you stay in the disused gold mine for the rest of the day and don't go back to Maintown until sunfall.

Good for you, partner – some things are more important than winning a rodeo. You haven't completed the quest, but you're an excellent human being.

Go back to the start of the book to try again, or turn to page 224 to make a different choice.

When you enter Snake Valley, you're surprised to find no snakes at all. It's just a big valley full of rocks.

"This place should be called *Rock* Valley," you chuckle, as Ancient Annie's Buffalo Farm appears in the distance. "Whoever named this place needs their eyes tested. There's not a single snake in the whole—"

HISSSSSSSSSSSSSSSSSSSSSSS!

The rocks move. A snake slithers out from each of them. They've been waiting for you to reach the middle of the valley and now you're surrounded. Tumbleweed is terrified. In fact, the poor mule is *so* scared she releases a little wind.

PARP.

Whoa, that smells worse than the Sheriff's boots!

Your eyes water, your nose runs, your face turns green. But somehow you manage to keep hold of Tumbleweed's reins until the air clears.

Blinking the tears from your eyes, you realise the snakes are still there. But they're lying on their backs with their tongues hanging out. Tumbleweed's whiffy wind has knocked them all senseless.

Yee-haw!

Quickly, you gallop to the other side of Snake Valley to escape the serpents and see a small wooden building near a field full of buffalo. An old woman is digging potatoes. When she sees you approaching, she throws her trowel onto the soil and runs towards you.

"Bless my buffalo!" she cries, pulling you out of your saddle and flinging her arms around your neck. It's meant to be a hug, but it feels more like a wrestling contest. "You're the first person I've seen in years! *Years!* No-one ever dares go around Grey Rock to visit Ancient Annie! Oh gee, I sure am pleased to see you!"

The old woman has quite a grip.

"I...can't...breathe," you tell her.

"Sorry," she says, releasing your neck. "Now, what can I do for you, kid?"

"I'm on a quest to cure the Sheriff's horse," you tell her. "I'm looking for some buffalo milk. Do you have any?"

"Of course," she replies, "anything for my new friend. But first, won't you come in for a cup of tea and a chat? Did I mention it's been years since I've seen anyone?"

To go inside for a cup of tea, turn to page 239.
To politely refuse and get on with your quest, turn to page 236.

You make a dash for the cactus patch on the back of your trusty mule and with a roar the lion gives chase. He's closing in on Tumbleweed's tail, despite your speedy head-start, and as you skid between the cacti he lifts his enormous paws and pounces.

"MEEYOWCH!"

Silly lion. He wasn't looking where he was going and now he's scratched himself on one of the plants. You feel a bit sorry for him, but you're also glad he's running across the desert with his tail between his legs.

That was a close call, partner!

Breathing a sigh of relief, you gaze around at the plants. Who knew there were so many types of cactus? Some have needles like thorns, some have prickles like hairs, some have beautiful flowers like giant butterflies, and one of them looks a bit like Mrs Bullwinkle from the Maintown Store.

You can learn more about cactus plants in Great Grandpappy Pete's notebook. Would you like to take a look?

Yes, please, I love cactus plants. Turn to page 248.

No, thanks. I really couldn't care less about cactus plants. Turn to page 245.

Climbing out of your saddle, you peer down at the mega-bird to find a man's face staring out of the feathers.

"At *last!*" cries the man. "I thought I'd be stuck in this mud forever!"

"Crikey," you say, "who are you? And why are you wearing those feathers on your head?"

"It's a disguise," he explains, "to fool the birds. Pull me out of here and I'll introduce myself." You do as he asks and the man takes off his disguise. "The name's Rogers. Professor Rogers. I've been camping in Green Woodland with that pompous idiot of a scientist, Horatio Smythe. We're here to study the wildlife."

"Horatio Smythe? You mean that hermit I bumped into earlier on?"

"He's no hermit," says Professor Rogers. "Horatio Smythe is the Queen of England's third cousin twice removed and he's incredibly self-absorbed. Last Friday, I left our tent to study a flock of Silver-Feathered Goose chicks. I've been stuck in that mud ever since and I bet Horatio hasn't even noticed I'm missing."

"You've been out here for *five days?*" you gasp.

"You must be starving."

"Ravenous," nods the professor. He points at the mule. "Is that a dragon fruit sticking out of your saddlebag?"

"Oh, yes, it is, but—"

Before you can stop him, the professor snatches the fruit and shoves it into his mouth, skin and all. You watch in horror as the last dribble of it runs down his chin.

"Delicious!" he smiles. "Thanks so much, old fellow. Tell you what, let's ditch that self-important scientist and I'll treat you to a slap-up meal at the Maintown saloon."

Cripes! Professor Rogers has eaten one of your ingredients. You don't have time to go back to the cactus patch for another dragon fruit. Plus, none of the professor' feathers came from a Four-Legged Duck. Oh well, at least you're getting a free meal after all your hard work.

Well done for finding two ingredients, heroic StoryQuester – you should be mighty pleased with yourself!

StoryQuest over. Go back to the start of the book to try again.

"I'm really sorry about your dog," you tell Crabbity Jack. "Here, take these coins and buy him a sweater. I've only got four, but you can have them all."

"LABRADOR?" scowls the old farmer, wiggling his finger in his left ear. "ROVER AIN'T NO LABRADOR. HE'S A GOLDEN RETRIEVER."

"I said, you can *have them all*," you reply. You place the gold coins in Crabbity Jack's hand. "To buy a sweater for your dog."

"YOU WANNA BUY MY DOG?"

"No, that's not what I'm saying—"

"FOUR GOLD COINS AIN'T GONNA BUY MY ROVER. BUT THROW IN THE MULE AND WE'VE GOT A DEAL."

Crabbity Jack leads Tumbleweed to the buffalo field then throws you off his land. The old mule will have lots of grass to graze on and plenty of animal friends to play with, so you shouldn't feel too sad. Plus, you have your bald dog to comfort you now.

Go back to the start of the book to try again, or turn to page 283 to make a different choice.

Tumbleweed moves slowly away from the hermit and you pass by unnoticed, still holding the divination stick in the air.

"This stick is a waste of time," you tell the mule. "We only fell into that river because I wasn't looking where I was going. I'm getting rid of it," and you throw it over your shoulder.

SPLASH!

The divination stick has landed in a small woodland stream (how does it *do* that?). The water is moving at speed and you trot alongside it until you reach a small clearing.

A gently bubbling waterfall trickles into a sparkling lake, nestled amongst the trees like a hidden diamond. There are tall reeds on the far side and a cluster of lily-pads in the middle, and there, floating and playing and messing around on the lake, are hundreds, no, *thousands* of birds!

There are red birds, green birds, fat birds, thin birds, tall birds, short birds, birds with beaks, birds without beaks (no, wait, those are frogs), and there, hiding amongst the reeds, there's a really strange-looking bird with totally mismatched feathers. It's like someone has taken a single feather from each of the other birds and sewed them together to make one giant mega-bird.

If there's a Four-Legged Duck to be found, surely *this* is the place to find it. But the birds' feet are all underwater. How will you find out if any are the species you're looking for?

If you want to check Great Grandpappy Pete's notebook for clues, turn to page 285.
If you want to take a closer look at the mega-bird, turn to page 305.

"That's okay," says the Sheriff, "you don't need the star to enjoy the rodeo. Come on, partner, let's go."

This year's celebrations are the best you've ever seen. There are people in fancy-dress, a sheep-herding contest, a ragtime band playing your favourite songs, line-dancing groups, yummy food and the most popular riding contest this side of Blue River – the grand barrel-race.

All the best riders have travelled across the Wild West to compete. They saddle-up and gallop around two barrels, in and out of the obstacles as fast as their horses will carry them, and the quickest time wins. But of course, no-one ever beats the Sheriff and his fine horse, and that's all part of the fun.

At the end of the competition, Lightning Bolt is awarded a big rosette and the Sheriff tells everyone about his incredible stablehand, who crossed deserts and climbed mountains to save his trusty stead.

A huge cheer goes up as you and Tumbleweed take your place next to the Sheriff.

"I've been thinking," he says, as the crowd go crazy, "a Wild West explorer like you shouldn't be shovelling horse poo for pocket money – how would you like to be my Deputy instead?"

"No more poo-shovelling!" you cry. "Amazing!"

And later that evening, as the reddening sun sinks into the distant horizon, you walk Tumbleweed back to her shed with your shiny new Deputy's badge.

"Gee," you tell your four-legged friend, "this sure has been a mighty fine adventure."

Tumbleweed releases a little wind, and you're pretty sure what she means by that is...

"Yee-haw!"

Congratulations! You've completed the Sheriff's challenge and you're the new Deputy Sheriff of Maintown!
If you want to find the ultimate ending to your story, go back to the start of the book and try again.

Great Grandpappy's Pete's notebook has helped you find your next ingredient. Dragon fruits grow on cactus plants and there's one right there in front of you.

Yee-haw!

But the fruit is tucked between the spiny leaves of the cactus. If you scratch yourself you could end up with Itchity Fever, just like the Sheriff's horse, so you'll have to take care when picking it.

There's a rock on the sand. You could throw it at the dragon fruit to knock it down. Or you could use an animal bone to part the prickly leaves and carefully reach in.

Which would you like to do?

To use the rock, turn to page 314.
To use the bone, turn to page 294.

After checking Great Grandpappy Pete's notebook, you realise only two birds on the lake have striped feathers.

One is a small duck hiding under a low-hanging branch. It's sat on a nest, so you can't tell how many legs it has without taking a closer look.

The other is the mega-bird. At least some of its feathers are stripy, but you're not sure if any of them are *exactly* like Great Grandpappy Pete's drawing.

Which bird is most likely to be the Four-Legged Duck?

To take a closer look at the bird on the nest, turn to page 233.
To check out the mega-bird, turn to page 305.

You pick up a rock to throw at the dragon fruit, to find a scorpion hiding underneath it. The critter is startled, his tail twitches, and…

"Youch!"

Oh, no! You've been stung!

The scorpion's sting is venomous and your hand swells up to twice its normal size. It's so painful you almost pass out. You'll need to go back to Maintown to have it checked out, but try the challenge again when you've seen the doctor.

Go back to the start of the book to try again, or turn to page 312 to make a different choice.

The Wilderness Store has a sign on the door saying NO BANDITS, RUSTLERS OR DONKEYS ALLOWED. Luckily, you're none of these things, so you climb out of your saddle and enter the building.

Rows of wooden shelves line the walls. They're covered with fresh groceries, like cabbages, cauliflowers, parsnips and carrots. A middle-aged lady in a chequered dress is standing behind the counter.

"Welcome to the Wilderness Store," she says. "What can I get for you?"

"I'm on a quest to cure the Sheriff's horse," you tell her, "and I'm looking for a pint of—"

But suddenly, Tumbleweed barges into the shop and chomps down a huge mouthful of carrots.

CHOMP!

"You can't bring a donkey in here!" cries the shopkeeper. "Didn't you see the sign?"

You're embarrassed, so you try to lighten the mood with an amusing reply.

"I saw it," you say, "but she's not a donkey – she's a mule."

The woman doesn't find you funny, and now Tumbleweed has moved onto the cabbages.

CHOMP!

"Get that mangy creature out of my store!" cries the woman. "Or go somewhere else for your shopping!"

What do you want to do?

If you're unhappy with the customer service at the Wilderness Store and want to try Crabbity Jack's Shack instead, turn to page 235.

If you appreciate the Wilderness Store's attention to health and safety, and want to put Tumbleweed outside, turn to page 272.

Great Grandpappy Pete's Map of the Wild West

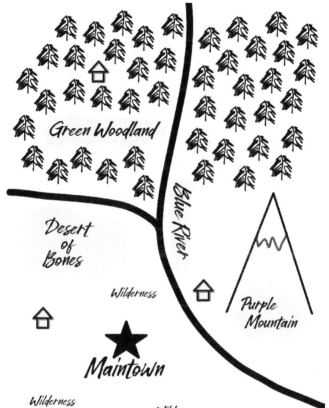

Green Woodland

Blue River

Desert
of
Bones

Wilderness

Purple
Mountain

★
Maintown

Wilderness

Wilderness

Snake
Valley

Grey Rock

Dead Man's
Gorge

StoryQuest

CHOOSE THE PAGE - UNLOCK THE ADVENTURE

COLLECT THEM ALL!

Laugh along with Billy, as he boosts his brain to the size of Venus in this hilariously gruesome chapter book also by Becci Murray.

Or try these very serious poems about really important stuff (like sausages, yaks and toenails) in this illustrated collection of rhyming silliness.

Becci Murray is a British author from Gloucestershire. She used to run a children's entertainment company, where she earned a living playing musical bumps and doing the Hokey Cokey (true story). Her favourite books are by Roald Dahl and she has a life-size BFG sticker on her bedroom wall (well, almost life-size).

You can learn more about Becci or send her a message by visiting the Llama House Children's Books website – she would love to hear from you!

www.llamahousebooks.com

Printed in Great Britain
by Amazon